'You *lied* to me?'

'I wouldn't exactly call it ███████████████ expected surprise—incre███████████████ of the day a ski instructo███ ████ ████ swapped for a billionaire. He had taken it as a given that his newly discovered status would do its usual job and bring a smile of servile appreciation to her lips. It hadn't.

'Well, *I* would.' Milly was struggling to contain her anger. How *dared* he? How dared he play her for a complete fool?

'You made false assumptions,' Lucas told her with barely concealed impatience. 'I chose not to set you straight.'

She sprang to her feet and stormed over to the window, stared out for a little while, and then stormed back towards him, hands on her hips. 'Why didn't you just tell me who you were?'

Because I was enjoying the novelty of being with someone refreshingly honest... Because in a world where wariness and suspicion are bywords it was a holiday, not having to guard every syllable, watch every turn of phrase, accept instant adulation without being able to distinguish what was genuine and what was promoted by a healthy knowledge of how much I was worth...

'When you're as rich as I am, it pays to be careful.'

'In other words, I could have been just another cheap, tacky gold-digger, after your money?'

'If you want to put it like that…'

His darl█████████████████████████████████e could ha███

But ther███████████████████████████████████s him.

3011780157261 7

Cathy Williams can remember reading Mills and Boon® as a teenager, and now that she's writing them she remains an avid fan. For her, there is nothing like creating romantic stories and engaging plots, and each and every book is a new adventure. Cathy lives in London, and her three daughters, Charlotte, Olivia and Emma, have always been and continue to be the greatest inspiration in her life.

Books by Cathy Williams

Seven Sexy Sins

To Sin with the Tycoon

Protecting His Legacy

The Secret Sinclair

One Night In…

His Christmas Acquisition

The Uncompromising Italian
The Argentinian's Demand
Secrets of a Ruthless Tycoon
Enthralled by Moretti
His Temporary Mistress
A Deal with Di Capua
The Secret Casella Baby
The Notorious Gabriel Diaz
A Tempestuous Temptation
The Girl He'd Overlooked
The Truth Behind His Touch
Her Impossible Boss

**Visit the author profile page at
www.millsandboon.co.uk for more titles**

THE REAL
ROMERO

BY
CATHY WILLIAMS

Published in Great Britain 2015
by Mills & Boon, an imprint of Harlequin (UK) Limited,
Eton House, 18-24 Paradise Road, Richmond, Surrey, TW9 1SR

© 2015 Cathy Williams

ISBN: 978-0-263-24849-4

Harlequin (UK) Limited's policy is to use papers that are natural,
renewable and recyclable products and made from wood grown in
sustainable forests. The logging and manufacturing processes conform
to the legal environmental regulations of the country of origin.

Printed and bound in Spain
by CPI, Barcelona

THE REAL ROMERO

To my fabulous and inspiring daughters.

CHAPTER ONE

'AMELIA? IS THAT Amelia Mayfield?'

Milly pressed the mobile phone against her ear, already regretting that she had been stupid enough to pick up the call. How many more instructions could Sandra King give about this job?

She was going to be a chalet girl! Two weeks of cooking and looking after a family of four! Anyone would think that she was being primed to run the country. It wasn't even as though she hadn't done this before. She had, two years ago, for three months before she'd started the hotel job in London.

'Yes.' She sighed, allowing her eyes to drift over the pure, dazzling canvas of white snow all around her. It had been a fantastic trip, just the thing to clear her head and get her mind off her miserable situation. She had travelled in style and she had enjoyed every second of it. It was almost a shame that she was now in the back seat of the chauffeur-driven SUV with her destination only half an hour away.

'You haven't been picking up your phone!' The voice down the other end was sharp and accusatory. Milly could picture the other woman clearly, sitting at her desk in Mayfair, her shiny blond hair scraped back with an

Alice band, her long perfectly manicured nails tapping impatiently on her desk.

Sandra King had interviewed her not once but three times for this job. It was almost as though she had resented having to give the job to someone small and round with red hair when there were so many other, more suitable candidates in the mix: girls with cut-glass accents, braying laughs and shiny blond hair scraped back with Alice bands.

But, as she had made clear with unnecessarily cruel satisfaction, this particular family wanted someone plain and down to earth, because the last thing the *señora* wanted was a floozy who might decide to start flirting with her rich husband.

Milly, who had looked up the family she would be working for on Google after her first interview, had only just managed not to snort with disbelief because the husband in question was definitely *not* the sort of man any girl in her right mind would choose to flirt with. He was portly, semi-balding and the wrong side of fifty, but he was filthy rich, and she supposed that that was as compelling an attraction as being a rock star. Not that she was in the market for flirting with anyone, anyway.

'Sorry, Sandra...' She grinned because she knew that Sandra didn't like being called by her first name. It was 'Ms King', or 'Skipper' to the chosen few. The other girls in the exclusive agency that dealt specifically with part-time positions to the rich and famous called her Skipper, one of those silly nicknames that Milly guessed had been concocted in whatever posh boarding school they had all attended.

'The service has been a bit iffy ever since I left London...and I can't talk for long because my phone's al-

most out of charge.' Not strictly true but she didn't need
yet another check list of the various things the special
family ate and didn't eat; or the favourite things the special little kids, aged four and six, insisted on doing before they went to bed. She didn't need to be reminded of
what she could and couldn't wear, or say or couldn't say.

Milly had never known people to be as fussy with
just about everything. The family for whom she had
worked two years previously had been jolly, outdoorsy
and amenable.

But she wasn't complaining. They might be fussy
but the pay was fabulous and, more importantly, the
job removed her from the vicinity of Robbie, Emily
and heartbreak.

She had managed to push her ex-fiancé, her best
friend and her broken engagement out of her head, but
she could feel them staging another takeover, and she
blinked rapidly, fighting back tears of self-pity. Time
healed, she had been told repeatedly by her friends,
who had never liked Robbie from the start and, now
that she was no longer engaged, had felt free to let loose
every single pejorative thing they had thought about
him from day one.

On the one hand, their negative comments had been
bolstering and supportive. On the other, they had shown
up her utter lack of judgement.

'In that case,' the well-bred, disembodied voice informed her, 'I'm afraid I have to inform you that the
job has been cancelled.'

It took a few seconds for that to sink in. Milly had
been busy being distracted by the unfortunate turn
of events that had catapulted her life from sorted and
happy to humiliated and up in the air.

'Did you hear what I just said, Amelia?'

'You're kidding, aren't you? Please tell me that this is a joke.' But Sandra King was not the sort who had a sense of humour. Any joke, for her, would be foreign territory.

'I never joke,' the other woman said, on cue. 'The Ramos family has pulled out at the last minute. I only took their phone call a few hours ago and, if you had *picked up your phone* instead of *letting it ring,* you would not have wasted your time travelling.'

'Why? Why is it off?' Visions of slinking back into the flat she had shared with Emily, risking bumping into her one-time best friend clearing her stuff before she took off to America with Robbie, were so horrifying that she felt giddy.

'One of the kids has come down with chicken pox. Simple as that.'

'But I'm only half an hour away from the lodge!' Milly all but wailed.

They had left the exclusive village of Courchevel behind and the car was wending its way upwards, leaving the riff-raff of the lower slopes behind as it entered the rarefied air of the seriously rich. Hidden, private lodges with majestic views; helipads; heated indoor swimming pools; saunas and steam rooms by the bucket load...

There was an elaborate sigh from the end of the line. 'Well, you'll have to tell the driver to swing round and head back, I'm afraid. Naturally, you will be compensated for your time and trouble...'

'Surely I can spend *one night* there? It's getting dark and I'm exhausted. I have a key to the place. I can use it and make sure that I leave the lodge in pristine condition. I need to sleep, Sandra!'

She couldn't get her head round the fact that the one thing that seemed to be working in her favour, the *only* thing that had worked in her favour for the past couple of horrific, nightmarish weeks, was now collapsing around her feet like a deck of cards, kicked down by one of the odious rich kids from the family who had bailed at the last minute. A wave of hopeless self-pity threatened to engulf her.

'That would be highly irregular.'

'So is the fact that my job here has been cancelled at the last minute, when I'm *fifteen minutes* away from the lodge—having spent the past eight hours travelling!'

She could see the lodge rearing up ahead of them and for a few seconds every depressing, negative thought flew from her head in sheer, wondrous appreciation of the magnificent structure ahead of her.

It dominated the skyscape, rising up against the blindingly white snow, master of all it surveyed. It was absolutely enormous, the largest and grandest ski lodge Milly had ever seen in her life. In fact, it was almost an understatement to classify it as a 'lodge'. It was more like a mansion in the middle of its own private, snowy playground.

'I suppose there's little choice!' Sandra snapped. 'But for God's sake, Amelia, pick up when you hear your phone! And make sure you don't touch anything. No poking around. Just eat and sleep and make sure that when you leave the lodge no one knows you've been there.'

Milly grimaced as she was abruptly disconnected. She leaned forward, craning to get glimpses of the mansion as it drew closer and closer to her, until the SUV was turning left and climbing through private land to where it nestled in all its splendour.

'Er...' She cleared her throat and hoped that the driver, who had greeted her at Chambery airport in extremely broken English and had not said a word since, would get the gist of what she was going to say.

'Oui, mademoiselle?'

Milly caught his eye in the rear-view mirror. 'Yes, well, there's been a slight change of plan...'

'What is that?'

She sighed with relief. At least she wouldn't have to try and explain an impossible situation using her limited French, resisting the temptation to fill in the gaps by speaking loudly. She told him as succinctly as possible. He would have to stay overnight somewhere and return her to the airport the following day... Sorry, so sorry for the inconvenience, but he could phone...

She scrambled into her capacious rucksack and extracted her wallet and from that the agency card that she had not envisaged having to use for the next couple of weeks.

She wondered whether he might stay at the lodge, it was big enough to fit a hundred drivers, but that was something he would have to work out for himself. She suspected that she had already stretched Sandra's limited supply of the milk of human kindness by asking if she could stay overnight in the place.

It was a dog-eat-dog world, she thought. As things stood, she was rock-bottom of the pack. She had been cheated on by her fiancé, a guy she had known since childhood and, as if that wasn't bad enough, she had been cheated on by her best friend and flatmate...

To top it off, she had been told that the reason he had become engaged to her in the first place was because his parents were fed up with his twenty-four-seven lifestyle of living it large and womanising. They had given him a deadline to find himself a decent girl and settle down or else he could forget about taking over the family business that had just opened a thriving branch in Philadelphia and was going places.

Banished from the family fortune and a ready-made job, he would have been faced, she assumed, with the terrifying prospect of actually buckling down and finding himself a job without Mummy and Daddy's helping hand. And so he had plumped for the slightly less terrifying prospect of charming her into thinking that they really had a relationship, proposing marriage whilst playing the field with her much taller, much skinnier and much prettier flatmate.

His parents had approved of her. She had passed the litmus test with them. She was his passport to his inheritance. She was small, round and homely; when she thought of Robbie and the angular Emily, every insecurity she nursed about her looks rose to the surface at the speed of light.

The only thing worse than catching them in bed together would have been actually marrying the creep, only to discover once the ring was on her finger that he had zero interest in her.

She gazed mournfully at her finger where a giant diamond rock had nestled only a few weeks ago.

Her friends had all told her that it was a monumental mistake to have chucked it back at him, that she should have kept it and flogged it at the first available opportunity. After all, she deserved it, after what he had put her through.

And the money would have stood her in good stead, considering she had jacked in her hotel job so that she could play happy families with him in Philadelphia. It was galling to think that he had had the nerve to tell her that he hoped she understood and that she could count on him if she ever needed anything!

As things currently stood, she was out of a job, banished from her flat until Emily cleared out and with a shockingly small amount of money saved.

And she had no one to turn to. Her only living relative, her grandmother who lived in Scotland, would have sold her cottage had she known about her granddaughter's state of near penury, but Milly had no intention of filling her in on that. It was bad enough that she had had to pick up the pieces when she had been told fifteen days ago that the fairy-tale wedding was off the cards.

As far as her grandmother was concerned, Milly was taking time off to work as a nanny for a family in Courchevel, where she would be able to do what she loved most, namely ski... She had glossed over the trauma of her breakup as just one of those things, nothing that a couple of weeks in the snow couldn't cure.

Milly had painted a glowing picture of a cosy family, practically friends, who would be there for her on her road to recovery. It had helped her grandmother to stop fretting. Furthermore, she had embroidered the recovery theme by announcing that she had another job lined up as soon as she was back in London, far better than the one she had jettisoned.

As far as her grandmother was concerned, she was as right as rain, because the last thing Milly wanted to do was worry her.

'Shall I call...er...the agency and see if you could stay overnight at the lodge...?' Her better instincts grudgingly cranked into gear and she resigned herself to another awkward conversation with Sandra, who would probably spend a ridiculously long time telling her that being let down was all her fault because she should have just *answered her phone,* having confirmed that the driver would not, definitely *not,* be allowed to sully the mansion, no way.

But, no; Pierre, the driver, was a regular at one of the hotels in Courchevel, where one of his relatives worked, and he would be fine there.

Milly was tempted to ask whether being let down by the special family came with the job. Maybe he had a permanent room there for when he got messed around.

She didn't. Instead, she allowed him to help her with her luggage, the luggage containing the clothes that would never be worn, and he only drove off when she had unlocked the imposing front door to let herself into the lodge.

It was blessedly warm and indescribably stunning, a testimony to the marvels of modern architecture and minimalism. The entire space was open-plan, with two sitting rooms cleverly split by a wall in which a high-tech, uber-modern fire caught the eye and held it. Beyond that, she could glimpse a vast kitchen, and beyond that yet more, although she was drawn to the floor-to-ceiling windows that captured the spectacular views of the valley.

She gazed out at the untouched, pristine snow, fast fading as night descended. It had been an excellent ski season so far—good accumulation of snow, which had collected on the roofs of the lodges lower down the mountain and lay there like banks and banks of smooth, marzipan icing.

Having no idea of the layout of the lodge, she decided to take her time exploring. She wasn't going to be there long, so why not enjoy the adventure of discovery? Her flat was small and poky. More than four people in the sitting area constituted a traffic jam. Why not pretend that this place belonged to her?

She explored each room exhaustively, one at a time. She admired the sparse, expensive furnishings. She had never seen so much chrome, glass and leather under one roof in her life before. Much of the furniture was white, and she marvelled at a couple confident enough to let loose two small children in a space where there was so much potential for destruction.

The kitchen was a wonder to behold: black granite counters, a table fashioned from beaten metal and an array of gadgets that made her culinary fingers itch.

She decided that she was glad she no longer worked at the Rainbow Hotel. It boasted three stars, but everyone there reckoned palms must have been greased to get that rating because the rooms were basic, bordering on the criminally dull, the restaurant should have been updated half a century ago and the two bars were straight out of the seventies but without a cool, retro feel.

Not to mention the fact that she had never been allowed, not once in a year and a half, to do anything on her own, Chef Julian, whilst only dabbling in the actual cooking, had specialised in peering over her shoulder and picking fault with her cooking whenever he got the chance.

Here, she could have let her imagination go wild—within the constraints of the various faddy food groups they did and didn't eat, of course. She trailed her hand over the gleaming, spotless counter and brushed a few of the marvellous gadgets, none of which bore the hallmarks of anyone ever having been near them. When she checked the fridge, it was to find that it was fully stocked, as were the cupboards. A horizontal metal wine rack groaned under the weight of bottles, all of which bore expensive, fancy labels.

Absorbed in her inspection of the kitchen, daydreaming about what it might feel like actually to have enough money to own a place like this as a second home, Milly was unaware of anyone approaching.

'And you are…?'

The deep, cold voice coming from behind crashed through her pleasant, escapist fantasy with the unwelcome force of a sledgehammer and she spun round, heart pounding.

Her brain, which had been lagging behind, caught up to point out mockingly that there was a stranger in the house and she should be looking for something handy with which she could defend herself.

Because the man could be….*dangerous*…

Her mind went blank. She forgot that she should be scared—terrified, even. She was in a bloody great rolling mansion packed full of valuables and the owners weren't there. The man standing in front of her, all six foot something of him, had probably broken in. She had probably disturbed him in the middle of ransacking the place, and everyone knew what happened to innocent people when they happened to interrupt a robbery.

But, God, had she ever seen someone so beautiful?

Raven-black hair, slightly longer than was conventionally permissible, framed a face that was, simply put, a thing of perfection: a wide, sensual mouth; chiselled features; eyes as dark and as fathomless as night. He was in jeans and a T-shirt and was barefoot.

It seemed unusual for a robber to take his shoes off to make off with the silver, but then it occurred to her that he had probably removed them so that he could sneak up on her unannounced.

'I could ask you the same thing!' She tried to keep the tenor of her voice calm and controlled—a woman in charge of the situation, someone who wasn't going to be intimidated. 'And don't even *think* of taking a single step closer to me!' Idiot that she was, she had left her mobile phone lying in her rucksack, which was currently reclining on the kitchen counter. It was infuriating, but how could she possibly have anticipated something like this?

In stark disobedience of her orders, the man took a couple of steps closer to her and she fell back, bumped into the counter and spun round to grab the nearest heavy thing to hand—which happened to be the kettle, a glass concoction that didn't look as though it could stun a flea, never mind the muscled man who was now only a metre away from her and had folded his arms, cool as a cucumber.

'Or else what? Don't tell me you have plans for using that thing on me...?'

'You'd better tell me what you're doing here or else I'm going to...call the police. And I'm not kidding...'

This had not been the way Lucas had anticipated his evening going. In fact, he hadn't actually banked on being here at all. He had lent the place to his mother's annoying friends, only for them to cancel at the last minute, which was when he had decided to head there himself for a few days.

He would get away from his mother, who was becoming more strident in her demands for him to settle down and get married. She had suffered a minor stroke three months previously, had been pronounced fit and able, yet had decided that she had stared death in the face, had become acquainted with her own mortality—and now all she wanted was to hold a grandchild in her arms before she died. Was that asking too much of her only beloved son?

Frankly, Lucas thought that it was, but he had not

been inclined to say so. Instead, he had wheeled out consultant after consultant, but no amount of reassurances from these top consultants could convince her that her fragile grasp on life wasn't about to be snipped.

Add to that an annoying ex-girlfriend who refused to believe that she had been dumped, and a few days' skiing had suddenly seemed like a brilliant idea.

Bracing conversations with his mother could be better faced after he had vented his frustrations in a few black runs.

Peace and quiet seemed to have nosedived, however, and he was not in the best of moods to be standing here, staring down a crazy woman brandishing his kettle and threatening to call the police.

A short, crazy woman, with red hair that was all over the place, and who thought he was looting the place. Hilarious.

'You don't really think you could take me on, do you?' With lightning reflexes, he reached out and relieved her of her dangerous weapon, which he proceeded to set back down on its base. 'Now, before *I* call the police and have you forcibly removed, you're going to tell me what the hell *you're* doing here.'

Deprived of the kettle, Milly stuck her chin out at a stubborn angle and stared at him defiantly. 'You're not scaring me, if that's your intention.'

'It's never been my intention to scare a woman.'

The man oozed sex appeal through every pore. It was off-putting. How could she get her thoughts in order when he stood there, looking at her with those darker-than-night eyes that were insolent and intransigent at the same time? How was she supposed to *think*?

'I'm actually *employed* here.' Milly broke the silence. A thin film of perspiration had broken out over her body and, try as she might, she couldn't seem to peel her eyes away from him.

He raised one enquiring eyebrow, and she glared at him, because she had every right to be here which he, almost certainly, did not.

What, she wondered, could possibly go wrong next? How could one person's life get derailed in such a short space of time? She should have been here recovering, looking forward to an essential break from normality while she mentally gathered her forces and rallied her troops in preparation for returning to London. She should have been using the splendid kitchen to whip something up that was gluten-free for Mrs Ramos, meat-based for her husband and healthily braised for their children! Instead, she was having a staring match with someone who looked like Adonis but behaved like a caveman.

'Oh, yes?'

'Yes,' she snapped. '*Not* that it's any of your business! I'm the chalet girl the Ramos employed to work for them for the next two weeks. And they'll be here *any minute now...*'

'Ah...chalet girl... Now, why am I finding that hard to believe when I know for a fact that Alberto and Julia won't be here because one of their children is ill?' He strolled over to the fridge and helped himself to a bottle of mineral water, which he proceeded to drink while keeping his eye on her.

'Oh.' The annoying, arrogant man wasn't a robber but, instead of rushing to reassure her, he had prolonged her discomfort by not deigning to tell her that he knew the family who owned the lodge. Were there *any* nice guys left in the world? 'Well, if you think that I'm going to apologise for...for...'

'Coming at me with the kettle?'

'Then you're mistaken. I don't know what you're doing here, but you shouldn't sneak around, and you should have told me that you knew the owners...' A thought occurred to her. 'I suppose they've let you down, as well?'

'Come again?'

'They let *me* down,' Milly expanded glumly. Now that she was no longer in danger of imminent attack, her breathing had more or less returned to normal, but she still found that she had to put a little distance between her and Adonis, who was still standing by the fridge and yet managing to have a very weird effect on her nervous system.

His legs, she noted absently as she sat down on one of the high-tech leather-and-chrome chairs by the table, were long and muscular and he had good ankles. Not many men had good ankles but he had excellent ones—brown like the rest of him...with a sprinkling of dark hair...

She surfaced to find that he had said something and she frowned.

'Not you, as well.' She groaned, because from the tail end of his sentence she gathered he had been pointing out the obvious—which was how it was that she had managed to make the trip without being notified that the job had been cancelled. 'I've had enough lecturing from Sandra about not picking up my phone; I don't think I have the energy to sit through you telling me the same thing. Anyway, why are *you* here? Didn't your agency let you know before you made a wasted trip here?'

Lucas had the dazed feeling of someone thrown into a washing machine and the spin cycle turned to full blast. She had raked her fingers through her wild red hair, which he now appreciated was thick and very long, practically down to her waist, a tumbling riot of curls and waves.

'Agency?' Never lost for words in any given situation, he now found himself speechless.

'Sandra's the girl at the agency that employed me. In London.' She permitted herself to look at him fully and could feel hot colour racing up to her face. He was obviously foreign, beautifully and exotically foreign, but his English was perfect, with just a trace of an accent.

'My job was to cook for the Ramos family and babysit their children.' It suddenly occurred to her that he had called them by their Christian names. She had been under strict instructions to use their full titles and to remember that they weren't her friends. It just went to show how different agencies operated; just her luck to have got stuck with snooty Sandra. 'What were *you* employed to do? No, you don't have to tell me.'

'I don't?' Fascinating. Like someone from another planet. Wherever Lucas went, he generated adulation and subservience from women. They tripped over themselves to please him. They said what they imagined he wanted to hear. Born into wealth, he had known from a tender age what the meaning of power was and now, at the ripe young age of thirty-four, and with several fortunes behind him—some inherited, the rest made himself. He was accustomed to being treated like a man at the top of his game. A billionaire who could have whatever he pleased at the snap of his imperious fingers.

What did this woman think he did? He was curious to hear.

'Ski instructor.' Milly discovered that this strange turn of events was having a very beneficial effect on her levels of depression. Robbie, Emily and the horror story that had suddenly become her life had barely crossed her mind ever since Adonis had appeared on the scene.

'Ski instructor.' He was parroting everything she said. He couldn't believe it.

'You have the *look* of a ski instructor,' Milly said thoughtfully.

'Am I to take that as a compliment?'

'You can if you want.' She backtracked hastily just in case he got it into his head that she was somehow trying it on with him, which she wasn't, because aside from anything else she was far too upset even to look at another man. 'Isn't it amazing how rich people live?' She swiftly changed the topic and watched, warily, as he dumped the bottled water on the counter, making no effort even to look for the bin, and sauntered towards the kitchen table so that he could sit on one of the chairs, idly pulling another towards him with his foot and using it as a foot rest.

'Amazing,' Lucas agreed.

'I mean, have you had a chance to look around this place? It's like something from one of those house magazines! It's hard to believe that anyone actually ever uses this lodge. Everything's just so…shiny and expensive!'

'Money impresses you, does it?' Lucas thought of all the other apartments and houses he owned, scattered in cities across the world from New York to Hong Kong. He even had a villa on an exclusive Caribbean island. He hadn't been there for at least a couple of years…

Milly leaned on the table, cupped her chin in the palm of her hand and gazed at him. Amazing eyes, she thought idly, with even more amazing lashes—long, dark and thick. And there was a certain arrogance about him. She should find it a complete turn-off, especially

considering that Robbie had had his fair share of arrogance, and what a creep he had turned out to be. But
Adonis's arrogance was somehow *different*... Just look
at the way he had stuck his feet on that chair.

'No...' she admitted. 'I mean, don't get me wrong,
money is great. I wish I had more of it.' *Especially considering I have no job to return to.* 'But I was brought
up to believe that there were more important things in
life. My parents died in a car accident when I was eight
and my grandmother raised me. Well, there wasn't an
awful lot of money to go round, but that never bothered
me. I think people create the lives they want to live and
they do that without the help of money...'

She sighed. 'Stop me if I'm talking too much. I do
that. But, now that I know you're not a burglar, it's kind
of nice having someone here. I mean, I'll be gone first
thing in the morning, but... Okay, enough of me... Is
this the first time you've worked for the Ramos family?
I mean, I couldn't help noticing that you called them by
their first names...'

Lucas thought of Alberto and Julia Ramos and
choked back a snort of derisive laughter at the thought
of working for them. In actual fact, Alberto had worked
for his father. Lucas had inherited him when his father
had died and, because of the personal connection, had
resisted sacking the man, who was borderline incompe-
tent. He found them intensely annoying but his mother
was godmother to one of their children.

'We go back a way,' he said, skirting round the truth.

'Thought so.'

'Why is that?'

Milly laughed and it felt as though this was the first
time she had laughed, really laughed, for a long time.
Well, at least two weeks, although there had been a mo-

ment or two with her friends post-traumatic break-up. Manic, desperate laughter, probably...

'Because you've got your feet on the chair and you've just dumped that empty bottle on the kitchen counter! Sandra told me that under *no circumstances* was there to be any sign that I'd stepped foot in this lodge when I left. I might even have to wipe all the surfaces just in case they find my fingerprints somewhere.'

'You have a wonderful laugh,' Lucas heard himself say with some surprise. She did. A rich, full- bodied laugh that made him want to grin.

And looking at her...

That first impression of someone small and plump with crazy hair was being rapidly dispelled. She was small, yes, barely skimming five-four, but her skin was satiny smooth and her eyes were the clearest blue he had ever seen. And when she laughed she had dimples.

Milly went bright red. In the aftermath of her horrible, *horrible* broken engagement, her self-confidence had been severely battered, and his compliment filled her with a terrific sense of wellbeing. Even if he had only complimented her on the way she laughed, which, when you analysed it, was hardly a compliment at all. But, still, coming from Adonis...

'Must be great being a ski instructor,' she said, all hot and bothered now. 'Would you like to know something? I mean, it's no big secret or anything...'

'I would love to know something...even if it's no big secret or anything...' Hell, this impromptu break was certainly proving to be a great distraction in ways he had never anticipated.

'I used to ski—I mean *really* ski. I went on a school trip when I was ten and somehow I took to it. When I was fifteen, I even thought I might try and go pro, but you know… We didn't have the money for that sort of thing. But it's why I was looking forward to this job…'

Her situation hit her like a blast of cold air: no fiancé, no job, no two weeks' chalet income with the bonus of skiing now and again. She shook away her sudden despondency, which wasn't going to get her anywhere. 'Frankly, it's why Sandra employed me in the first place when there were other better looking girls lining up for the job.' *That and my low levels of physical attractiveness.* 'I thought I might be able to sneak a little skiing in, but now… Oh, well, that's life, I guess. My luck's been crap recently so I don't know why I'm surprised this fell through.'

She smiled, digging deep to recover some of her sunny nature. 'Hey, I don't even know your name! I'm Amelia, but my friends call me Milly.' She held out her hand, and the feel of his cool fingers as he shook it sent a wave of dizzying electric charge straight through her body, from her toes to the top of her head.

'And I am…Lucas.' So she thought he was a ski instructor. How frankly refreshing to be in the company of a woman who didn't know his worth, who didn't simper, who wasn't out to try and trap him. 'And I think we might just be able to solve the matter of your lost job…'

CHAPTER TWO

IT WAS A SPUR-OF-THE-MOMENT decision for Lucas, but whoever said that he wasn't a man who could think creatively on his feet? How many times had he won deals because he had approached them from a different angle; played with a situation, found the loopholes, cracks and crevices and exploited them to his own benefit? It was the crucial difference between moderate success and soaring the heights. He had been bred with confidence and it had never once occurred to him that he might not be able to get exactly what he wanted.

Right now, he had made the snap decision that he might enjoy the woman's company on the slopes for a few days.

She obviously wasn't the type he normally went for. His diet was tall, thin, leggy brunettes from social backgrounds very similar to his own—because there was nothing worse than a tawdry gold-digger—but she had a certain something...

Just at this minute she was gaping at him as though he had taken leave of his senses.

'I beg your pardon?' Milly could scarcely believe her ears. In fact, she was on the way to convincing herself that she was trapped with a madman. He might be well in with the Ramos family if he happened to be their personal ski instructor, but how much influence did ski instructors have anyway? It wasn't as though they weren't disposable.

'But first, food.'

'Food?'

'I actually came to the kitchen to grab myself something to eat.' Originally he had toyed with the idea of just importing a chef from one of the hotels, the regular chef he was accustomed to using whenever he happened to be at the lodge, but in the end it had hardly seemed worth the effort when he hadn't planned to stay longer than a couple of nights. And when he knew for a fact that the fridge would be brimming over with food in preparation for the non-appearing Ramos family.

'You came here to grab something to eat? Are you completely *crazy?* You can't just go rummaging around in their fridge, eating their food and drinking their wine. Have you taken a look at the bottles in that wine rack? They look as though they cost the earth!'

Lucas was already heading for the fridge.

'Bread…' He opened the fridge door and turned to look at her. 'Cheese… Both in plentiful supply. And I'm pretty sure there'll be some salad stuff somewhere.'

Milly sprang to her feet. 'I can, er, cook you something if you like…if you're sure. After all, cooking *was* to be part of my duties.'

Lucas looked at her and smiled and that electric charge zipped through her again. It was like being struck by a bolt of lightning.

Had Robbie the creep ever had this effect on her? She didn't think so, but then again disillusionment might have put a different spin on her memories of their somewhat brief courtship.

She and Robbie had attended the same small school in remote Scotland until they were fourteen, at which point grander things had beckoned and he had moved with his family down to London. At fourteen, gauche and way too sporty to appeal to teenage boys whose testosterone levels were kicking in, she had had a secret crush on him.

They had kept in touch over the years, mostly via social network with the occasional visit thrown in whenever he'd happened to be in the city, but his sudden interest in her had only really kicked off six months ago and it had been whirlwind. Milly, still finding her feet in her job, had been first pleased to see a familiar face and then flattered when that familiar face had started take an interest in her. Ha! The reason for that had become patently clear after he had dumped her for leggy Emily.

Lucas had slammed shut the fridge in favour of opening a bottle of the expensive wine from the wine rack, much to Milly's consternation.

So, women cooking for him had never been part of the deal; tinkering in the kitchen smacked of just the sort of cosy domesticity he had never encouraged. On the other hand, this was a unique situation.

'I'm actually a chef by profession.' Milly grinned and joined him by the fridge, the contents of which she proceeded to inspect, although she made sure not to remove anything. She could practically feel Skipper Sandra peering down at her, about to ask her what the hell she thought she was doing.

'Would-be professional skier, chef… Is there no end to your talents?'

'You're teasing me.' Their eyes met and she blushed. 'I still don't feel entirely comfortable digging in their cupboards but I suppose we *do* have to eat. I mean, I'm sure Sandra wouldn't expect me to *starve*...'

'This Sandra character sounds like a despot.' Lucas removed himself from her way as she began extracting bits and pieces. He had no idea what she intended to do with the stuff. He himself had zero interest in cooking and had never really seen fit to do much more than toast a slice of bread or, in dire circumstances, open a can of something and put it in a saucepan.

'Like you wouldn't believe.' She began hunting down utensils whilst reminding him, just in case he reported back that she had made herself at home, that she still didn't feel 100 percent good about using stuff from their fridge. 'Want to help?' She glanced over her shoulder to where he was lounging indolently against the kitchen counter with a glass of red wine in his hand.

Talk about making himself at home!

'I'm more of a spectator when it comes to cooking,' Lucas told her. And from where he was standing, the view was second to none. She had removed her thick jumper and was down to a clingy long-sleeved T-shirt that outlined every inch of a body that had been woefully kept under wraps.

'We'll eat quicker if you help.'

'I'm in no hurry. You were about to tell me about Sandra the despot...'

'I had to have three interviews for this job. Can you believe it? Three! The Ramoses are just about the fussiest people on the planet. Oh, sorry; I forgot that you're their regular ski instructor. You probably see a different side to them.' She sighed, her throat suddenly thick as she thought of the neatly packaged life she had been looking forward to flying through the window.

And yet, in a strange way, she was sure that she should be feeling sadder than she actually was.

Mortified, yes. She was about eleven out of ten on the mortification scale, although less so here where her well-meaning friends weren't hovering around her, hankies at the ready, as though she was on the verge of a nervous breakdown.

But sad?

The presents had all been returned; the dress had been sold online because the shop had refused to have it back; the small church in Sunningdale where his parents had lived ever since they had moved from Scotland had been cancelled. But she didn't get a lump in her throat when she thought about the details.

The lump came when she thought about the fairytale future she had had planned, when she thought about being in love and then being let down...

'I doubt that.' Lucas recalled the last time he had seen the couple at his mother's house in Argentina, where Julia Ramos had spent most of the evening lording it over anyone she thought might be a lesser mortal.

Despite being wealthy beyond most people's wildest dreams, his mother had a very solid streak of normality in her and frequently hosted parties to which all and sundry were invited, regardless of their income or status. She had never forgotten that both she and his father had come from nothing and had made their fortune through hard graft.

'There aren't many complex sides to Alberto and Julia Ramos. They have money and they insist on showing the world, whether the world wants to know or not.'

'Poor you.' Milly looked at him sympathetically. 'I guess it must become a bit of a drag if you're having to deal with people you don't especially like...' She returned to her chopping and he dragged one of the bar stools over so that he could see her as she worked. By now, she had given up on being appalled at the liberties he took. Perhaps that was the relationship he had with his employers. Less of an employee and more of an equal.

'But,' she continued as she tried to focus on the onions in front of her and ignore the fact that his dark eyes roving over her were making her feel a bit dizzy, 'we all have to do stuff we don't particularly like for the sake of earning a living. What do you do when you're not instructing?'

'This and that.'

Milly didn't say anything. Maybe he was embarrassed because being a ski instructor might be glamorous but it was hardly a ladder-climbing job, and she wasn't sure why, but Lucas struck her as the kind of guy to have ambition.

'Why are you doing a two-week stint as a chalet girl when you're a professional chef? You're not drinking your wine. You should. It's an excellent vintage.'

'I hope you don't get into trouble opening that bottle…' But the cooking was now done so she wiped her hands on one of the towels by the range, took the proffered glass of wine and followed him out of the kitchen and into the sprawling sitting area, where, through the vast panes of glass, they could see the spectacular sight of night settling on the snowy mountain ranges.

'I never get into trouble,' Lucas assured her as he joined her on the sofa. The white sofa. The white sofa that she would probably have to pay for if she made the mistake of spilling her red wine on it.

She perched awkwardly on the edge and made very sure to keep a firm hand on the stem of her wine glass.

'You *never* get into trouble…ever? That's a very arrogant thing to say!' But strangely thrilling.

'I confess that I can be arrogant,' Lucas told her truthfully, eyes steady on her face as he sipped his wine.

'That's an awful trait.'

'Deplorable. Have you got any?'

'Any what?' Her glass appeared to be empty. How had that happened?

'Deplorable traits.' Not red, he decided; her hair was not red…more a deep, rich auburn with streaks of lighter auburn running through it.

'I tend to fall for creeps. In fact, you could say that I specialise in that. I went out with boyfriend number one three years ago for three months. Turned out he had a girlfriend, who happened to be doing a gap year leaving him free to play the field while she was away…'

'The world is full of creeps,' Lucas murmured. He himself always made it very clear to the women he dated that rocks on fingers were never going be part of the game. If, at any point, they got it into their heads that they could alter that situation, then they were very sharply brought up to date with his ground rules.

'You're not kidding.'

'And boyfriend number two?'

'Boyfriend number two was actually my fiancé.' She stared at her empty glass, wondering whether she dared risk another drink. She wouldn't want to face the trip back to London on a hangover. She sneaked a glance at Lucas, who was reclining on the leather sofa, utterly and completely comfortable in his surroundings.

'Fiancé?'

Milly stuck her hand out for inspection. 'What do you see?'

Lucas shifted position, leaned forward and looked.

'An extremely attractive hand.' He glanced up at her and was charmed by the dainty colour in her cheeks.

'It's a hand without an engagement ring,' she said mournfully. 'Right now, at this precise moment in time, I should actually be a married woman.'

'Ah...'

'Instead, here I am, drinking wine that doesn't belong to me—which the Ramos family will probably discover and report back to Sandra the despot—and pouring my heart out to a complete stranger.'

'Sometimes complete strangers make the best listeners.'

'You don't strike me as the sort of guy who pours his heart out to other people.'

'It's not a habit I've ever actively encouraged. Tell me about the ex-fiancé...'

Milly thought that she had spent the past two weeks offloading about the ex-fiancé. Her friends had been fertile ground for endless meandering conversations about Robert and *types* like Robert. Over boxes of wine and Chinese take-out, hours had been spent discussing every aspect of Robert and men in general. Anecdotes of various Mr Wrongs had been cited like a never-ending string of rabbits being pulled from a magician's hat.

'You're not really interested...' She couldn't see *him* ever going through the trauma of being dumped from a great height.

'You fascinate me,' Lucas murmured, reaching over to the bottle, which he had casually dumped on one of the spotless glass tables so that he could refill both their glasses. Milly noted that the bottle had left a circular stain on the table and she mentally made a note to make sure it was wiped clean before she went to bed.

'I do?' She decided that that rated slightly higher than the compliment he had paid her about her laugh.

'You do,' Lucas told her gravely. 'I have never known anyone as…open and forthcoming as you.'

'Oh.' Deflated, Milly looked at him. 'I suppose that's just a kind way of saying that I talk too much.'

'You also have amazing hair.'

Was he *flirting* with her? Milly made her mind up that there was no way that she would allow herself to be flattered, especially not by a ski instructor who probably slept with every woman he taught over the age of twenty. Weren't they notorious for that? The last time she had worked as a chalet girl, the other two girls who had also been working with her had both had flings with ski instructors. Ski instructors were usually young, cute, unnaturally tanned and extremely confident when it came to enticing women into bed.

She shot him a jaundiced look, which was not the reaction he expected on the back of a compliment. He wondered how she would react if he told her that what he would really like to do, right here, right now, was sift his fingers through that wonderful hair of hers and watch it as it rippled over them.

'So what was the ex called?'

'Robert,' Milly told him on a sigh. Determined to make this glass last as long as possible and thereby avoid any nasty early-morning consequences, she took a miniscule sip.

'And what did *Robert* do?'

'Fell into bed with my best friend. Apparently he took one look at her and realised that he couldn't resist her. It turned out that he had proposed to me because I fitted the bill. His parents wanted him to settle down and I was *settling down* material. But not in a good way.

More in an "if he could do as he pleased, he wouldn't settle down with me" sort of way. He thought his parents would approve, which they did.'

She sighed and swallowed a more robust mouthful of wine. 'He said he really *liked* me, which is the biggest insult a girl could have, because he obviously wasn't actually that attracted to me. At any rate, he must really have fallen for Emily because he braved his parents' wrath to tell them about her and now...what can I say? She'll be having the life I had planned on having.'

'Married to a bastard who will probably find another skirt to chase within two years of getting hitched? I wouldn't wallow in too much self-pity if I were you...'

Milly laughed. To the point. Where her friends would spend literally hours analysing, he had cut to the chase in a few sentences.

'And now shall we see how that food of yours is doing?' Lucas stood up and stretched and Milly tried not to let her mouth fall open at the ripple of muscle discernible under his clothes.

'Yes, the food; the stolen food.'

'And I shall make a few calls; do something about this job of yours that's disappeared under your feet.'

Milly hadn't forgotten about that but she had decided not to mention it again. People had a way of saying stuff they seriously meant at the time but five minutes later had completely forgotten. Sometimes she had been guilty of that particular crime. A wide, sweeping invitation to friends to come round for drinks only to realise afterwards that she would actually be at work on the evening in question.

'You're going to make a few calls?'

'Two, in actual fact.' He watched her cute rear as she preceded him into the kitchen. He knew more about her life after five seconds than he had about anyone he had dated in the past, but then he didn't naturally encourage outpourings, and the women he dated were all too conscious of the fact that they had to toe the line. No outpourings. No long life stories. No involved anecdotes.

Was it any wonder that he was frankly enjoying himself? He would never have imagined that being a ski instructor could be such a liberating experience. He wondered whether he shouldn't become a ski instructor for a week every year just so that he could refresh his palate with a taste of normality.

He disappeared, heading back to the sitting room so that he could make his calls as he stood absently looking down at the sprawling white vista outside his lodge.

One call to his mother, to tell her that he might be staying on slightly longer than originally thought. The other to Alberto, to tell him that his chalet girl had arrived to find herself jobless and that he would be digging into his pocket to pay her what she was due, because she would be staying on, and that he should contact whatever agency he got her from and relay the message. Lucas could easily have afforded to pay her himself but on principle he saw no reason why he should pick up the tab. The man was grossly over-paid by his company for what he did, and Lucas suspected that he had told the agency that the deal was off at the last possible minute because neither he nor his wife would really have given a damn if their chalet girl's nose was put out of joint.

He sauntered into the kitchen, snapping his phone shut just as she was dishing out two heaped bowls of pasta.

'Done.'

Alone and away from his overpowering personality, Milly had had a little while to consider the prospect of spending two weeks with a man she didn't know in a lodge that belonged to neither of them. The plan made no sense. Were they to deplete the contents of the fridge? Guzzle all the alcohol? Then leave with a cheery wave goodbye? Wouldn't a bill catch up with her sooner or later? There was no such thing as a free lunch, after all, not to mention two weeks' worth of free lunches.

And, also, what if the ski instructor with the drop-dead good looks turned out to be dodgy? He didn't seem the violent type but who was to say he was trustworthy? He could be a gentleman by day and a sex maniac by night.

Bracketing Lucas and sex in the same thought brought hectic colour to her cheeks. Even if he *was* a closet sex maniac, there was no chance he would look twice in her direction. Robert, who had been nice looking but definitely not in Adonis's league, hadn't found her attractive. That, in a nutshell, said it all as far as Milly was concerned.

But she still found herself hesitating, clearing her throat and sitting down at the sleek kitchen table with burning, self-conscious hesitation.

Would it be inappropriate to ask him for a CV? she wondered. Maybe a few references from women he had happened to be thrown together with inadvertently who had found him to be a decent, honourable man with upstanding moral values?

'The look of joy and satisfaction seems to be missing from your expression.' Lucas tucked into the pasta, which was as good as anything he had had in any restaurant. He had wondered about the 'professional chef' description of herself—had thought that maybe it was a bit of self-congratulation when, in fact, she worked behind the scenes at the local fast food joint—but she was a seriously good cook.

'Well....' Curiosity got the better of her. 'How did you manage to do that? I mean when you say *done...*'

'You'd be surprised at the things I can accomplish when I put my mind to it. Your job here is safe, and you'll be fully paid for the duration. Even if you decide to leave after two days.'

Milly's mouth dropped open and Lucas grinned wryly.

'Admit it. You're impressed.'

'Wow. You must have an awful lot of influence with the Ramos family.' A thought struck her and she went bright red and took refuge in her pasta.

'Why do I get the feeling that there's something on your mind?' Lucas drawled drily.

'What makes you think that?'

'Maybe it's because you've suddenly turned the colour of puce. Or maybe it's because you have a face that's as transparent as a pane of glass. Pick either option. The food's delicious, by the way. Were it not for the red hair, I would be tempted to think that you have a streak of Italian running through you.'

'Auburn, not red. I don't like the word "red",' Milly automatically asserted, still staring down at her plate.

'Spit it out, Milly of the "auburn not red" hair...'

'Well, you probably wouldn't like it.'

Lucas helped himself to more pasta, poured himself another glass of wine and allowed the silence to stretch between them. Eventually, he rescued her from her agonising indecision.

'Trust me, I'm built like a brick wall when it comes to being offended.' Not that he could think, offhand, of anyone who would dare say something offensive to him. The joys of wealth and power.

'You really *are* arrogant, aren't you?' Milly said distractedly and he delivered her a slashing smile that temporarily knocked her for six. 'Well, if you must know, I just wondered whether you managed to pull strings because you're sleeping with Mrs Ramos…' She said it in one rushed sentence and then held her breath and waited for a reply.

For a few seconds, Lucas didn't actually believe what he had just heard and then, when it *had* sunk in, he wasn't sure whether to be outraged, amused or incredulous.

'Well…' She dragged that one syllable out, licking her lips nervously. 'It makes a weird kind of sense.'

'In what world does it make a weird kind of sense?'

'How else would you be able to get me my job and ensure that I get paid for it?'

'Ski instructors can have a lot of influence, as it happens.' Lucas skirted over that sweeping and vague statement because it was one thing to delicately economise on the truth and another to lie outright, especially to someone who, he suspected, had probably never told so much as a white lie in her entire life. 'I've helped Alberto out on a number of occasions and, put it this way, he was more than happy to do as I asked. Furthermore, I would never go near a married woman.'

'You wouldn't?'

'Don't tell me—all the ski instructors you've met have been more than obliging with women whether they were wearing wedding rings on their fingers or not?'

'Their reputations *can* be a little racy.' But she breathed a sigh of relief. 'Just one other small thing…'

'You *do* take testing conversations to the outer limits, don't you?'

'I wouldn't normally…er…choose to be alone in a ski lodge with someone I actually don't know.'

This time Lucas *was* outraged. He flung his hands in the air in a gesture that was mesmerising and typically foreign and leaned back into his chair. 'So, not only do you clock me for a womaniser who doesn't bother to discriminate between single and married women, but now I'm a pervert!'

'No!' Milly squeaked, on the verge of telling him to keep his voice down because, with all the food and wine they had consumed, guilt was making its presence felt in a very intrusive way. It would be just her luck to find out that he hadn't made any phone calls at all, that he was in fact a burglar who had decided to make himself at home before getting down to the serious business of nicking the silver, and to top it off somewhere lurking behind a wall was Sandra and her band of blond-haired guard dogs.

'How do I know that you've actually spoken to Mr Ramos?'

'Because I just told you that I had.' Unaccustomed to having his word doubted, Lucas was finding the conversation more and more surreal. 'I can prove it.'

'You can? How?' She cast him a dubious look. What was it about the guy? Her instinct was just to believe everything he told her, zombie-style. She was pretty sure that if he pointed to the sky and told her that there were spaceships hovering she would be more than half-inclined to wonder if they contained little green men.

Lucas dialled a number on his cell phone and, when it connected, spoke rapidly in Spanish and then placed the mobile on the table and put it on speakerphone.

Then he sat back, a picture of relaxation, and spoke. Very slowly and very clearly. Without taking his eyes off her face. Which, when inspected in-depth, as he was now doing, was really an extraordinarily attractive face. Why was that? She didn't have the sharp, high cheekbones of a model, nor did she have the haughty, self-confident air of a trust-fund chick, but there was just something soft yet stubborn about her, sympathetic yet outspoken…

She was the sort of person who would never give in without a fight and for a few seconds he felt impossibly enraged at the unseen but much discussed ex-fiancé who had dumped her. He almost lost track of the conversation he was in the middle of having with Alberto, who, naturally, had adopted the usual tone of subservience the second he knew who was on the line.

Like someone pulling off a magic trick, Lucas waved to the phone and folded his hands behind his head as he listened to Alberto do exactly what he had been told to do, which, in actual fact, was simply to tell the truth.

Yes, of course she could stay on! On full pay. *No hay problema.* Furthermore, there was no need for her to replace any of the food eaten or wine drunk, nor was there any need to run herself ragged trying to keep the lodge clean. All that would be sorted at a later date. Meanwhile, he would be transferring her pay directly into her account, if she would just text him the details of her bank account, and furthermore there would be a bonus in view of the inconvenience she had suffered.

'I feel just terrible,' was the first thing Milly said as soon as Alberto had signed off, having wished her a very pleasant stay and apologised for any inconvenience caused.

'You feel terrible. You give new meaning to the word "unpredictable". What's that supposed to mean? Why do you feel terrible? I thought you would be leaping around this kitchen with joy! Face it, you don't have to return to London and risk bumping into your charming "best friend" and the loser ex…nor do you have to worry about money for the time being because you'll be paid for your stay here. You can take the time out you wanted and oh, what joy, you won't even have to slave over a hot stove catering to the Ramos family. In other words, you won't have to sing for your supper. From where I'm standing, you couldn't have wished for a better deal…yet you look as though someone's cancelled your birthday.'

'I haven't exactly been nice to poor Mr Ramos, have I?' She flung the rhetorical question at him in a voice laden with accusation.

'Have I encouraged that?'

'I made assumptions. I just thought that—because I had a list of a hundred different things I had to prepare for them individually to eat, and because I had so many strict instructions on what I could wear and what I couldn't wear, and what I could say and couldn't say—they were a pretty demanding, diva family. And yet…' She dug into her rucksack, grabbed her phone and texted the relevant information to Alberto.

'He couldn't have been more decent about the whole thing.' In record time she heard the ping of her phone as he confirmed that the money had been deposited into her account. 'After Robbie, it's nice to see that there are some decent people left in the world.'

Lucas was fighting down annoyance over Alberto and his ridiculous demands. He could kiss sweet goodbye to any further freebies at the lodge, whatever the family connection.

'So is the Dance of Joy and Happiness about to take place? Oh, no, I forgot, you still think that I'm a pervert you can't trust...'

'No.' Milly sighed. And anyway, had she really been conceited enough to imagine that he would make some kind of pass at her? Which was something she would obviously reject out of hand, because she was recovering from a broken heart! Not that he would anyway. Adonis types went for Aphrodite types—known fact.

'I'm weak with relief.'

'I guess we should clean here and then turn in for the night,' she said, standing up. The rollercoaster ride loosely called 'her life' was still looping her around in a million different directions. So now, unbelievably, she was staying on at the lodge for the full duration of her contract. From jobless and heading back on the first flight to still in work, earning her fabulous wage for two weeks of having fun and skiing...

'Clean?'

'Do the dishes.' She waved at the plates, the glasses, the saucepans. 'You might not be able to cook, but you can certainly help tidy this kitchen. I'm not doing it on my own. We both contributed to the mess.'

Lucas stood back, arms folded, and realised that 'do the dishes' had never been words applied to him, but he obligingly began clearing the table while she spent a little more time expressing completely unnecessary levels of remorse for having been uncharitable towards Alberto and his family.

As consciences went, hers appeared to be extremely overactive.

'Okay!' He held up one hand, cutting short yet another take on how kind the Ramos man had turned out to be. 'I get the general picture. Not,' he added darkly,

'that you actually know the first thing about Ramos…
er…Alberto… But no point going down that road.' He
leaned against the kitchen counter and folded his arms.

His contribution to tidying the kitchen had consisted
of moving two plates and a glass from the table to the
sink.

Good-looking men were always spoiled, first by their
adoring mothers, who ran around doing everything for
them, then by adoring girlfriends who did the same, and
finally by their adoring wives, who picked up where the
girlfriends had left off.

'Let's just cut short the Ramos eulogies. Now that
you're here, I'm going to be here for a couple of days.
We can talk about which runs we do.' She was someone
capable, by all accounts, of skiing to a high standard,
as opposed to dressing to a high standard with lamen-
tably average skiing skills, which had always been the
case with his girlfriends in the past. The actual process
of skiing had always been an interruption to the more
engaging business of looking good in skiing outfits.

A quirky, amusing companion who didn't know him
from Adam. Who knew what the outcome of their brief,
unexpected meeting of ways would be?

In his highly controlled and largely predictable life,
the prospect of the unknown dangled in front of him
like a tantalising carrot.

He smiled and closely watched the way she blushed
and lowered her eyes.

Yes, coming here had definitely been the right decision…

CHAPTER THREE

'SOMETHING'S ONLY JUST occurred to me...'

The dishes had been done, mostly by Milly, while Lucas had relaxed and fiddled with the complicated coffee-making machine, eventually succeeding in producing two small cups of espresso that she was embarrassed to tell him would probably keep her up all night. It had taken him such a long time finally to get there that it would have seemed churlish to politely refuse. She had never met anyone more clueless when it came to knowing his way around a kitchen. Or less interested, for that matter.

Now they were back on the white sofa although, with permission granted to stay in the lodge, she felt a little less uncomfortable in her surroundings.

'And I take it that this sudden thought is one you want to share with me.' This was a brave, new world. She had already berated him for not helping enough in the kitchen and had then proceeded to give him a mini-lecture on the wonders of 'the modern man'. Apparently those were men who shared all the domestic chores, cooked and cleaned with the best of them and gave foot massages to their loved ones. He had told her that, quite frankly, he could think of nothing worse.

'I should have asked you this before but with everything going on my mind was all over the place...'

Lucas grunted. The emails that he had planned to spend the evening ploughing through had quickly taken a back seat to the girl now staring off into the distance with a thoughtful frown.

'I should have asked you whether you're...er...involved with someone or not.'

'Involved with someone...'

'Are you married?' she asked bluntly. 'Not that it makes any difference, because we're both just employees who happen to be stranded in the same lodge.' *The same empty lodge.* 'But I wouldn't want your wife to be worried. You know...'

'You mean you wouldn't want her to be jealous.'

'Well, *anxious*...' So he *was* married, despite the lack of a wedding ring. Lots of men didn't wear wedding rings. She felt a stab of disappointment. Why wouldn't he be married? she thought, restlessly pushing aside that awkward, uninvited emotion that had no place in her life. He was sinfully sexy and oozed just the sort of self-assurance and lazy arrogance that women went wild for.

'Interesting concept. A jealous and anxious wife worried about her beloved husband sharing a ski lodge with a total stranger...' He tried the thought on for size and tried not to burst out laughing.

When it came to women and commitment, he was the least likely candidate. Once bitten, twice shy and he had had his brush with his one and only near-escape. It had been a decade and a half ago but as learning curves went it had been a good one. He had been a nineteen-year-old kid, already with plenty of experience but still too green to recognise when he was being played. He'd been young, cocky and arrogant enough to think that gold-diggers all came wrapped up and packaged the same way: big hair, high heels, obvious charms.

But Betina Crew, at twenty-seven nearly eight years older than him, had been just the opposite. She had been a wild flower-child who went on protest marches and waxed lyrical about saving the world. He had fallen hook, line and sinker until she'd tried to reel him in with a phoney pregnancy scare, which he had so nearly bought, and had so nearly walked down the aisle. It was pure chance that he had discovered the packet of contraceptive pills tucked away at the back of one of her drawers and, when he'd confronted her, it had all ended up turning ugly.

Since then, he had never kidded himself that there was such a thing as disinterested true love. Not when the size of his bank balance was known. His parents might have had the perfect marriage, but they had both started off broke and had worked together to make their fortune. His mother still believed in all that clap trap about true love, and he hadn't the heart to disillusion her, but he knew that when and if he ever decided to tie the knot it would be less Cupid's bow and arrow than a decent arrangement overseen by a lawyer with a watertight pre-nup.

'No.' He shook his head. 'No anxious, jealous or whatever-you-want-to-call-it wife keeping the home fires warm.'

'Girlfriend?'

'Why the interest? Are you suggesting that there might be something for a woman to be jealous about?'

'No!' Milly nearly choked on her espresso. 'In case you'd forgotten,' she added, regaining her composure, 'I came over here to try and escape. The last thing on my mind would be involvement with anyone! I just don't want to think that there's anyone out there who cares about you and who might be alarmed that we happen to be stuck here together through no fault of our own.'

'In that case, I'll set your mind at rest, shall I? No girlfriend and, even if there was a girlfriend, I'm not a jealous guy and I don't encourage jealousy in women I date.'

'How can you discourage someone from being jealous?' She hadn't been at all jealous when it came to Robbie. Why was that? she wondered. Was it because she had known him off and on for a long time, and one was never that jealous when it came to people they were familiar with? She hadn't even thought twice about Robbie and Emily being alone together. And yet there was something deep inside telling her that surely jealousy was something that attacked at random and couldn't be debated or ordered out of existence?

'I've never found a problem with that. The women I date know my parameters and they tend to respect them.'

'You're the most arrogant guy I've ever met in my entire life,' Milly said with genuine wonderment.

'I think you've already told me that.' He drained his cup and dumped it on one of the coffee tables, then he stood up and flexed his muscles, watching as she uncurled herself from the sofa and automatically reached to gather his cup along with hers.

His automatic instinct was irritably to tell her to leave it, that someone would tidy it away in the morning, then he remembered that there would be no cleaner trooping along to make sure she tidied in his wake.

'I'll show you to your room.'

'Feels odd to be here without the owner in residence.'

Lucas had the grace to flush but he refrained from saying anything, instead scooping up her holdall, which had seen better days, and heading out towards a spiral staircase that led up to a huge galleried landing that overlooked the ground floor.

There, as on the ground floor, soaring windows gave out to the same spectacular views of the open, snow-covered mountains. It was dark outside and the snow was a peculiar dull-blue white against the velvety darkness.

For a few seconds, Milly paused to admire the vista, which was truly breathtakingly beautiful. When she looked away it was to find his dark eyes speculatively pinned to her face.

She was here with a guy she didn't know and yet, far from feeling threatened in any way, she felt *safe*. There was something silent and inherently strong about him that was deeply reassuring. She felt that if the place were to be invaded by a clutch of knife wielding bandits he would be able to dispatch them single-handedly.

'I have no idea where Ramos was going to put you,' Lucas told her truthfully. 'But I expect this room will do as good as any of the others.'

He flung wide the door and she gasped. It was, simply put, the most splendid bedroom she had ever seen. She almost didn't want to disturb its perfection by going inside. He breezed in and tossed her bag on the elegant *chaise longue* by the window, yet another of those massive windows designed to remind you of the still, white, glorious silence that lay outside.

'Well?' Lucas rarely noticed his surroundings but he did now because the expression on her face was so tellingly awestruck.

Playground for the seriously rich—this was what

the lodge was. He had had zero input into its decor. He had left that to a world famous interior designer. When the job had been done, he had dispatched three of his trusted employees to give it the once over and make sure that everything had been done to the highest possible standard, no corners cut. Thereafter he had used it a handful of times when the season was at its height and only if the skiing conditions were perfect.

It was a beautiful place. He looked at the cool, white furnishings, breathed in the air of calm, noted the quality of the wood and the subtlety of the faded Persian rug on the ground. Nothing jarred. In the bowels of the lodge, there was a comprehensive spa and sauna area. He'd used that once.

Now, he had an intense urge to take her down there and show it to her just so that he could see that expression of awe again, even though, regrettably, the lodge was not his as far as she was concerned. For the first time in living memory, he had an insane desire to *brag*. Hell, where had *that* come from?

'It's amazing.' Milly hovered by the door. 'Isn't it amazing? Well, I guess you're used to this, but I'm not. My entire flat could fit into this bedroom. Is that an *en suite* bathroom?'

Amused, Lucas pushed the adjoining door and, sure enough, it opened out to a bathroom that was almost as big as the bedroom and contained its own little sitting area. He wondered what the interior designer had had in mind when she'd decided on sticking furniture in the bathroom.

'Wow.' Milly tiptoed her way to the bathroom and peered in. It was absolutely enormous. 'You could have a party in here,' she breathed in a hushed voice.

'I doubt anyone would choose to do that.'

'How can you be so blasé about all of this?' She was too busy inspecting her glorious surroundings to look at him but she was acutely aware of his masculine presence next to her. 'I mean, do you teach lots of rich people? Is that it? You're accustomed to places like this because you're in them all the time?'

'I've been to a number of places along these lines...'

Milly laughed that infectious laugh that made him want to smile. 'Must be a terrific anti-climax when the season's over and you have to return to your digs.'

'I cope.'

Suddenly exhausted after a day of travelling and the stress of finding herself out of a job, then back in one, Milly yawned behind her hand and wandered over to her holdall, which was not the quality of bag that should have adorned the *chaise longue*.

'I've talked about myself all night,' she said sleepily. 'Tomorrow you can tell me all about yourself and your exciting life working for the rich and famous.'

A minute later she closed, and after a few seconds' thought locked, the bedroom door behind him and began running the bath. The ridiculously luxurious bath that was so big and so deep that it was almost the size of a plunge pool.

She wouldn't have believed it but she was having an impossible adventure and—okay, admit it—was so transfixed by Lucas that there had been no room in her head to feel sorry for herself.

She wondered what he did when he wasn't playing ski instructor to rich adults and their kids. Did he while away his summers in the company of wealthy socialites? He was good-looking enough to be a gigolo but she dismissed that idea as fast as it entered her head because she couldn't imagine that he could be that sleazy.

He'd said didn't sleep with married women and she believed him. There had been a shadow of repugnance when that suggestion had been mooted.

But he was a man of experience, from the way he had talked about the women he dated, in the casual voice of someone who was accustomed to getting a lot of attention and to dating a lot of women.

She thought about her own circumstances. When it came to experience with the opposite sex, she was wet behind the ears. She had never really been the kind of teenager who had become swept up in boys, in make-up, in short skirts and mini bottles of vodka at house parties. Maybe if she had had a mum; maybe if she hadn't been raised by her grandmother. She adored her grandmother, but she could reflect back and see that the generation gap had not been conducive to giggly conversations and experiments with make-up.

Nana Mayfield was a brisk, no-nonsense woman with a great love of the outdoors. Widowed at the age of forty-five, she had had to survive the harsh Scottish winters in unforgiving terrain and she had thrived. That love of the great outdoors was what she had brought to the relationship with her granddaughter and Milly had grown up loving all things to do with sport. She had followed sport on TV and had played as many sports as she could possibly fit into her school timetable.

Of course, she had been to parties, but hockey, tennis, rounders, even football, and later as much skiing as she could possibly do, had always come first.

And so the stages of infatuation, the teenage angst and disappointment, the adolescent broken hearts and the comparing of notes about boys with her friends, had largely passed her by.

Was that why she had fallen for Robbie in the first

place? Because her lack of experience had allowed flat-
tery and compliments to blind her to the reality of a relationship that was built on sand? Had a crush at fourteen
predisposed her to become the vulnerable idiot she had
been when he had swanned back into her life ten years
later? And then, had she held on to him because she
had wanted someone to call her own?

He hadn't even shown much interest in getting physical with her. How did that fit into the equation of two
love birds on the brink of a happy-ever-after life? And
she hadn't pushed him. That should have sounded the
alarm bells, but nope, she had merrily continued sleep
walking her way to the inevitable.

She had made sure to keep that to herself. She knew,
from listening to her friends, that they would all have
read the writing on the wall and would have known that
his only half-hearted attempts at touching her, and her
cheerful acceptance of that situation, did not augur a
healthy relationship. They had all been born and raised
in London and they were streetwise in ways she couldn't
hope to be.

She fell asleep to images of a dark, swarthy, sexy
face. He wasn't replacement therapy, but he was a distraction, and maybe that was exactly what she needed
right now: a harmless distraction.

The following morning it was snowing when she
awoke. She hadn't drawn the curtains and from the bed
she could look straight across to ceiling panes of glass
to the winter wonderland outside. She itched to put on
her skis and get out there.

Before she did anything, she telephoned her grandmother to tell her that she arrived safe and sound but
that the family in question had had a slight change of
plan, after which she managed to avoid directly lying

about her new circumstances, about sharing the lodge with a stranger. Then she texted her friends, brief texts telling them that she'd arrived. No more.

Once changed, she went downstairs and after prowling through the lodge finally located Lucas in a big, airy room behind a desk. She came to a halt outside the door and looked at him. There were papers spread around him and he was peering at a thin laptop computer, frowning.

'You're going to express concern that I'm sitting here without due respect for the owner, aren't you?' he said, without looking away from the computer.

He had had time to question his motives in offering her the use of his ski lodge. She was a young girl recovering from a broken relationship. In short, she was vulnerable and vulnerable, along with married, was something he didn't do.

Was he so jaded that he was prepared to try and take something simply because it made a change? And was a change as good as a rest? Yes, she was refreshing, as was the fact that she had no idea who he was or what he was worth, but was that any reason for him to amuse himself with her?

In any equation where 'vulnerable' appeared, hurt was always its companion.

He was immune but she wouldn't be. He knew what it was like to have complete control over the outcome of his emotional life, whilst she clearly didn't.

And yet…he couldn't escape the tempting notion that it would be utterly relaxing to spend a couple of days in her company. He could look without touching. It was called restraint and, whilst it was something he had never had any need to practise, it should be something that he could manage.

He needed to take time out from the combined stresses of his mother, who would not let up on reminding him that he needed to settle down, and an exgirlfriend who was still texting him in a way that was heading dangerously into stalker land. The fact that she knew his mother, albeit remotely, had foolishly led her to believe that their fling was more significant than what he'd had in mind.

He needed to take time out from being Lucas Romero. It was an elevated position he had occupied for his entire life. He had been born and bred to manage the family fortune and to add to it. He had never known what it felt like to be a normal person, with normal concerns. Wariness, suspicion, caution: those were the bywords in a life that was as wealthy and as powerful as his was.

'How did you know?' Overnight, Milly had wondered whether exhaustion and a build-up of stress were responsible for her exaggerating Lucas's overwhelming physical impact.

Not a bit of it. He was sprawled in front of his computer in all his devastatingly good-looking glory.

His near-black hair was swept back, accentuating the hard, chiselled lines of his face, and he was wearing a pale blue short-sleeved polo shirt that exposed the rippling, muscled strength of his arms and a glimpse of bronzed collarbone that made her mouth suddenly go dry.

'Because I'm getting the impression that you have a highly developed sense of guilt.' He stood up, dark eyes fixed on her face.

She was in a pair of jogging bottoms and a black base-layer long-sleeved T-shirt that clung to every curve of her small, sexy little body. It was just as well Ramos was not around. His wife would have spent the entire time trying to peel his eyes back into their sockets. The man was a notorious womaniser.

'What are you doing?'

Lucas logged off and leaned back, hands folded behind his head. 'Work.'

'Oh.' Milly looked at him, confused.

'A man has to get by.'

'What work?' Then her face cleared and she smiled. 'Oh, I remember. This and that. You didn't specify. How long have you been up?' It wasn't yet nine and he looked bright eyed and bushy tailed.

'I'm usually up by six.'

'Wow. Are you? Why?' Fascinated, she watched as he strolled towards her, pausing to stand directly in front of her so that she had to look up to him.

'What do you mean *why*?' Lucas asked, amused and puzzled.

'Why would you get up so early if you don't have to?' She felt breathless and exposed. 'I stay in bed as long as I can,' she confessed. 'Admittedly, my hours at the Rainbow Hotel are pretty long. *Were* pretty long. I'm out of a job now.'

She followed him towards the kitchen, chewing her lip, thinking about having to apply for more jobs as soon as she returned to London. How was she going to afford the rent on the flat? Emily would have disappeared off to her shiny new life that left her without a flatmate and with a disgruntled landlord. He might give her a little bit of leeway, if she explained the circumstances to him, but he wasn't a Good Samaritan and unless she found the rent money fast she would be out on her ear with nowhere to live.

'I like to be awake for as much of the day as possible,' Lucas murmured. Lie-ins were unheard of. Even if there was a woman in bed with him, he found it impossible to waste his time next to her, unless they were making love.

Sex got him into bed and kept him there. Sleep was something essential he had to grab. But, for him, those were the two main functions of a bed.

The kitchen was as they had left it. Milly stared around her, dismayed.

'You were up at six, made yourself a cup of coffee and yet you couldn't be bothered to tidy up?'

Lucas surveyed the kitchen as though seeing it for the first time. 'What's wrong with it?'

'Everything. The dishes need putting away…the counters need wiping…the milk's been left out…'

Lucas shrugged and looked at her with his head tilted to one side. 'I fail to see the point of tidying away anything that's going to make an appearance later on in the day. Same goes for the kitchen counters. Why wipe them? Unless you're planning on having a food-free day?'

'How can you be so blasé about someone else's property? You should respect the things that don't belong to you.'

'You're cute when you're being self-righteous,' he murmured and Milly stood stock still and folded her arms.

'You might think you're the hottest guy on the planet,' she said on an indrawn breath, 'and you might be bored because your job here with the Ramos family fell through, but that doesn't give you the right to flirt with me just because I happen to be around.'

'Who's flirting?' He surveyed her lazily. 'Simple statement of fact.'

'And I won't be running around cleaning up behind you like a maid either. I realise I'm being paid by Mr Ramos, who's been more than generous, all things considered—and I know that that's thanks to you—but I'm going to use my time here to really relax and try and forget about what I've been through. I don't want to feel as though I've got to be on full alert every time you're around.'

'I'm at a loss. What do you imagine I'm going to do?'

'Well, I just think we should lay down some boundary lines.'

'Agreed.' He held up both hands with a wicked grin that seem to utterly contradict what he had just said. 'Shall we have a spot of breakfast and then put our skiing skills to the test? The weather looks perfect. We could save the boundary line conversation for a little later.' He watched her hesitate, wondering whether to carry on the argument, maybe add to the 'boundary line' suggestion, but in the end the thought of taking to the slopes proved too much of a temptation and she smiled, her good humour restored.

Inexperienced.

Vulnerable.

He should be laying down more than just a few boundaries himself. He should be the one warning her off. He had the instincts of a born predator when it came to women and, however much she amused him, the last thing he wanted was for her somehow to get it into her head that he might be a worthwhile replacement for the vanishing ex-fiancé. The guy was obviously a complete loser, and she was well rid of him, but transference was a dangerous possibility and a complication he could do without.

As are women who have romantic notions of love and marriage, a little voice added. A complication he could do without...

Milly's face was flushed with happiness when, several hours later, they returned to the lodge.

The day's skiing had been exhausting, exhilarating, wonderful. It had been over a year since she had last taken to the slopes. The *real* slopes. She had managed to keep her hand in by going as often as she could to the nearest dry slopes, but nothing could come close to the feeling of euphoria when, poised at the very top of the mountain, you looked down to the naked, white beauty of snow-covered slopes. It was the closest you could get to your mind being empty, with just you and the infinite snowy space around you, your whole body yearning for the thrill of speed.

They had raced. She was good but he'd made her look like an amateur. He knew where to go to avoid all crowds. He would, she supposed. He would know these ranges like the back of his hand.

Dressed completely in black, including a black woolly hat and dark sunglasses, he was unbearably sexy, and she'd found her gaze drifting back to him repeatedly.

He moved as though he had been born to ski. He was skilled, fast, at times disappearing to reappear like a speeding bullet far ahead of her on the slopes.

They'd broken off for lunch at a tiny café nowhere near the hubbub of the town centre. This café was in the opposite direction, and there wasn't a single designer shop in sight—unlike the town centre, which heaved with rich and famous people spending money in the expensive shops that had sprung up to cater for their exclusive clientele.

Milly had loved it. She had never felt more relaxed as she'd sipped hot coffee and told him all about her childhood, her love of sports, the football team she supported. She'd told him about being brought up by her grandmother, the way it made you feel vulnerable to being left by the people you love.

It was weird but she knew that if she had met him under more normal circumstances there was no way she would ever have approached him. But here, things were different. She was recuperating from the humiliation of a broken heart, and he was the objective listening ear who didn't know her and so was not interested in tea and sympathy. In fact, he made no mention of Robbie except, when he could sense her drifting off, to tell her that the guy was a loser and she was better off without losers in her life.

'Tough times make you stronger,' had been his bracing observation when she had mentioned the uphill struggle of having to return to London to find work so that she could pay the rent on a house she couldn't really afford unless she found another lodger pronto.

Everything about him was as sexy as hell and by the end of the day she had stopped trying to pretend that she didn't want to just keep looking at him. She had stopped trying to figure out how it was that she could be broken-hearted and yet still open to his incredible, mind-blowing, raw animal magnetism...

Their joint love of skiing had banished her nerves. When she was moving on the snow, she was no longer the small, round red-haired girl who couldn't hold a candle to the tall glamorous models men found attractive. No, when she was skiing, she was at the top of her game and bursting with self-confidence.

* * *

Lucas had planned to stay no more than two nights at the ski lodge.

It was all the time he could spare. His high-octane life did not leave room for impromptu holidays. The impulse to go to the ski lodge where the isolation and privacy would recharge his batteries had been a good one.

The unexpected presence of Milly, her freshness and openness, had turned out to be even better for recharging his batteries.

By the second day, he had already made up his mind to take a couple more days off.

What was the point in having highly paid executives in place if you needed to hold their hand every time a decision had to be made? They could all do without him for a few days. Some of them could definitely do with an injection of backbone.

The truth was that he was enjoying himself. He was even enjoying his self-imposed rule of looking but not touching. He liked the way she coloured when he occasionally flirted with her. He liked the challenge of restraint when, the more he saw of her, the more he wanted to see. He liked her openness and he liked the way she confided, her pretty face pink and open and earnest.

The joy of restraint, however, was the certain knowledge that it could be broken at any given moment in time.

She fancied him. He had picked that up with finely tuned antennae: the way she sneaked sultry, stolen glances at him; the way she stilled whenever he got within a certain radius, as though ordering her body not to betray what she was feeling.

Her attempts to keep her distance were like constant

gauntlets being thrown down. His libido, jaded after a
diet of the same type of woman, was being tested to
its absolute limit.

It was invigorating.

It made him think that he had not faced up to any
sort of challenge for a very long time. He had flat-
lined. He made money, more than he could ever hope
to spend in a lifetime. He owned things and occasionally even enjoyed some of his possessions. And he had
women. However many he wanted and whatever variety he chose.

He was keeping his hands to himself but his deter-
mination to keep in mind that she didn't play by his
rules, that she had been hurt once and he didn't want
to be responsible for adding to the tally, was beginning
to fray round the edges.

Right now, she was downstairs cooking something.
It would be good. She would be moving around the
kitchen in clothes that showed off a body she seemed to
have downgraded to the lowest possible rating, despite
the fact there wasn't a red-blooded man on this earth
who wouldn't have appreciated those generous breasts,
that tiny waist and those womanly hips.

Wouldn't it do her good to have a man—a *real man,*
not a wimp like the vanishing ex—tell her how sexy
she was?

Wouldn't it do her self-confidence a power of good
for her to know what it felt like to be desired? From
what he had read between the lines, the ex had been a
waste of space from day one. They had met, gone to
the movies, gone on walks, enjoyed meals out. From
where he was standing, it had been a courtship that had
shrieked 'boring'—and most women with a little more

about them would have picked that up and moved on after deadly date number four.

But Milly hadn't and, now that fate had seen fit to bring them together for a few days, wouldn't he be doing her a *favour* if he showed her that she was a desirable woman? If he conclusively proved to her that she was well rid of the man, that she could have any guy she wanted…?

With the logical, clear-minded and concise brain any lawyer would kill for, Lucas made a mental list of all the many reasons why he could be justified in sleeping with her.

At the very end, he tacked on *no more restless nights for me wondering…*

He got downstairs to find the kitchen empty, with a note on the counter propped up against the salt shaker.

She had popped down to the town to get some stuff.

It had been snowing sporadically for the past twenty-four hours but the snow had gathered pace overnight. Optimum skiing conditions were bright-blue skies and good accumulation of snow. Too much falling snow could end up being inconvenient and, in some cases, downright dangerous to safe skiing.

He looked outside at what appeared to be a gathering snow storm. The lifts would be running at half-empty, if that. The line between safe and treacherous was slim. But she was a damned good skier. The best skiing companion he had ever had—courageous without taking unnecessary chances. He would wait for her to return and give himself a chance to catch up on work.

But there was no internet connection. Nor, when he tried his mobile phone, could he get a signal.

He waited a further twenty minutes and then realised that he had no choice but to hunt her down.

Chances were she was fine and on her way back but there was the very slender possibility that the sudden heavy snowfall had disorientated her, as it was wont to do with skiers unaccustomed to these slopes.

A disorientated skier very quickly became a skier at high risk. There had also been three avalanches in the past eighteen months. No casualties, but it only took one...

One disorientated skier, unfamiliar with the terrain, reacting without thinking, panicking...

When that happened, experience on a pair of sticks counted for nothing.

He dropped everything: the coffee he had just made; the historic files he had been about to review on his computer; the report waiting to be concluded.

He hit the slopes at a run, strapped himself into his skis and took off.

This was more than just a bit of fun for a couple of days. This was a serious case of *wanting* a woman and he was sick of playing mind games with himself. Hell, when he thought of her disappearing without him having bedded her...

He killed every single scruple that had been holding him back, because he was a man who was accustomed to taking what he wanted, and why bother trying to break the habits of a lifetime?

CHAPTER FOUR

THE GOING WAS slower than it would normally have been. Lucas was familiar with the slope down to the town centre but the thickly falling snow meant that he had to take it more carefully, which went against the grain when it came to skiing.

What the hell had she been thinking, venturing out when she must have known that there was the possibility of getting lost? She had never been here before and so far had only seen the slopes in his speeding wake.

He did his utmost to cover as much ground as possible, cross-skiing, eyes peeled for anything that might be a figure in distress. Or even a figure moving at a snail's pace, trying to get her bearings.

Nothing.

The slopes were virtually empty. The height of the tourist season was over and the falling snow would have kept most of the skiers indoors. Good food, good wine, expensive lodges—some, like his, with saunas and gyms. Being cooped up indoors would hardly be a hardship.

After twenty minutes, he saw the town approaching in the distance, a clutch of shops and restaurants, bars and cafés.

He hadn't planned to make this trip. He had planned

to stay put in the lodge, testing the less obvious ski slopes, maintaining his privacy. It was a small town and he was its wealthiest occasional visitor.

Cursing fluently under his breath, because he had no idea what 'stuff' she could possibly have needed to buy when the house was stocked with enough food for them to survive a sudden nuclear war, he resigned himself to a door-to-door search for her.

He hadn't signed up for this.

He was recognised within minutes of entering the first shop. He was stopped as he tried to progress through the town. His dark, striking looks halted people in their tracks, even those who didn't know who he was.

Somewhere, there would be someone with a camera. The place was a magnet for the paparazzi.

Hell! It made no difference to him whether some sleazeball with a camera snapped a photo of him but he would rather have avoided it. He valued his privacy, little of it as there was.

He found her in the very last café, huddled in front of a mug of hot chocolate, watching the snow storm. He had just spent the past hour trudging to find her and here she was, cool as a cucumber, sipping her drink without a care in the world!

He burst into the smart café and was, of course, immediately recognised by the owner. He might not have been a regular visitor but he was so extraordinarily high-profile that people went out of their way to garner his attention.

Even when, as now, he patently didn't want it. Especially not when she had spotted him and was frowning as she absorbed the café owner's deference.

The man was practically bowing as he retreated.

Lucas ignored him, choosing instead to hold her gaze as he strode towards her.

'What the hell do you think you're doing?'

'Enjoying a cup of hot chocolate.'

'Are you a complete idiot?' He remained standing, his face dark with anger. 'Have you noticed what's happening with the weather outside? Or are you in a world of your own? Come on. Let's go. Now!'

'Don't you dare order me around!'

Lucas leaned down, hands flat on the table, crowding her so that she automatically flinched back.

The café was half-empty but the few people there were whispering, looking covertly in their direction.

How dare he stride into this café and order her around like a schoolteacher telling a misbehaving kid what to do? *How dare he?* And where was the laid-guy who had listened to her rattle on about her life? The guy who had offered sparse but good advice, who had actually succeeded in helping her put her nightmare broken engagement into some kind of healthy perspective? Where had *he* gone? In his place, this was a dark, avenging stranger bossing her about, embarrassing her in front of other people.

Thanks to her lying, cheating ex-fiancé, she had spent the last two weeks smiling and putting on a brave face to mask her total humiliation. She wasn't about to let any stranger drag her back to that place!

'I am *not* ordering you around. I am very politely but very firmly telling you to drain the remnants of that hot chocolate and follow me out of here. Unless you want to find yourself spending the night in whatever hotel can fit you in!'

'I didn't ask you to come flying down here to rescue me!' Milly snapped, digging her heels in as a matter of principle, even though he was right. She had barely noticed the worsening weather. She should have. She knew all about worsening weather from growing up in Scotland—but she had been lost in her thoughts. 'And, for your information, it wasn't like this when I came out this morning.'

Lucas didn't answer. He pushed himself away from the table with the unswerving assumption that she would follow him, which she did.

'I haven't paid!' she gasped, catching up with his furious stride.

'There's no need to pay…' This from behind her.

Milly looked round, startled. 'Wh-what do you mean?' she stammered.

'Mr Romero is a very special visitor.' Like nearly every person working in the shops and cafés, the owner of this café was deferential to the wealthy and politely but condescendingly accommodating to everyone else. Money talked.

'A *very special visitor*…?' Milly's mouth wobbled on the brink of laughter because she wondered what a simple ski instructor could have done to have been awarded the title of 'very special visitor'. So he might have a handful of rich clients, but since when did their prestige rub off on him? Was he a *very special visitor* because of the way he looked?

'Enough, Jacques!' Lucas forced a smile but he could feel curiosity emanating from her in waves. 'Naturally your bill will be paid.' He turned to Milly. 'Did you have anything else? No? In that case, put it on my tab, Jacques.'

'Tab? What *tab*?'

She trailed out of the café behind him. The cable car was still in operation but for how long? Another hour and she might have been stranded downhill, unable to make her way back up to the lodge. 'I apologise if you felt you had to rush down to find me,' she offered grudgingly as they began the trip back up the hill. 'Like I said, conditions were a lot better when I started out.'

'And when they worsened, you intended to stay put, drinking hot chocolate and waiting for things to blow over?' Lucas turned to her, jaw clenched. 'I don't do rescue missions, so if you want to risk life and limb do me a favour and wait until I've vacated the lodge. Then you're more than welcome to take your life in your hands.' Not a very fair remark, but damn if he was going to retract it. When you went out to ski, you had to have your wits about you. One false move and you could end up endangering not just your own life but someone else's life, as well.

'I'm not responsible for you while you're out here,' he continued coldly.

'And I never asked you to be!' Her eyes flashed but he was right. She should have known better. That said, she had apologised, and he hadn't been big enough to accept it.

She turned away and stared off into the distance. What was it about her that was so poor when it came to reading men? Lucas had shown her a funny, charming side to him and she had been instantly captivated and disarmed. She'd have thought that experience, *very recent experience,* might have toughened her up a bit, made her just a little more jaundiced when it came to believing people and their motivations, but not so.

Apparently, he was fine when it came to her cooking for him and tidying up behind him like a skivvy. And if she wanted to chatter on inanely about herself, then he was happy enough to listen, because really, what choice did he have when he happened to be in the same room as her? But woe betide if she was stupid enough to think that any of those things amounted to him actually *liking* her.

She took people at face value. She always had. Growing up in a small town in remote Scotland where everyone knew everyone else had not prepared her for a world where it paid to be on guard. How many learning curves did one person need before they realised that having a trusting nature was a sure-fire guarantee of being let down? Especially when it came to the opposite sex?

Once back in the lodge, Milly stalked off to have a shower and get changed. The relaxed atmosphere between them had changed just like that after a silent trip back. She took her time having a very long bath and then changing into a pair of jeans and a comfortable cotton jumper. Her hair had gone wild in the snow and she did her best to tame it with the blow drier in the bathroom but in the end she resorted to tying it back in a loose braid down her back. Wisps and curly tendrils escaped around her face, but too bad.

For a few seconds, she looked at the reflection staring back at her in the mirror.

She couldn't remember ever having been envious of any of her friends when she had been growing up. They had been interested in cultivating their feminine wiles and getting with boys, and she hadn't. Not really. She hadn't been interested in make-up or skimpy clothes and she had been amused at how much time and effort some of her friends had devoted to their looks and to attracting boys. It had all seemed a bit of a waste of time, because they had all been in and out of relationships, spending half their time hanging around waiting for a text to come or else putting everything on hold because they were 'going steady' with a boy and somehow that left no time for anything else.

She was pretty sure that those girls would have matured into women who would be savvy enough to spot someone like Robbie for the fraud that he was—and would certainly have spotted Lucas for the arrogant kind of guy who thought he could say what he wanted and do as he pleased with the opposite sex.

He didn't *do* jealousy and he didn't *do* rescue missions and there were probably a million other things he *didn't do*. What it came down to was that he was someone who just did whatever he wanted to do and he didn't really care if he trampled on someone's feelings in the process.

It was not yet lunch time and the snow had already picked up a pace. Lucas was in the kitchen when she finally went downstairs, sitting at the table with a pot of coffee in front of him. Cut off from the outside world thanks to the snow storm, he had given up on trying to sift through paperwork he had brought with him.

She had sat in stony silence on their trip back, head averted, back rigid as a plank of wood as the cable car had carried them back up the slopes. There had been no pleading for him to listen to her and no trying to tempt him out of his foul mood. He had been spoiled by women who tiptoed around him. Despite her open, chatty nature, she was as stubborn as a mule.

'Perhaps I should have been a little less…insistent,' Lucas drawled, pushing aside the file he had given up on and watching the way she was deliberately avoiding eye contact with him. 'But you don't know this area and you don't know how fast and how severe these snow storms can be.' This was the closest he was going to get to an apology and it was a damn sight more than he would have offered anyone else.

'Is that your idea of an apology?' Milly asked, finally turning to look at him.

He must have showered during the time she had been upstairs, taking as long as she could in the bath without shrivelling to the size of a prune. His dark hair was slicked back and still damp, curling at the nape of his neck, and he was in loose grey jogging bottoms and a sweatshirt that managed to achieve the impossible—it was baggy and yet announced the hard muscularity of the body beneath it. He hadn't shaved and his jaw was shadowed with stubble.

He looked insanely gorgeous, which made her feel even more of a fool for having been sucked into thinking that he was Mr Nice. Since when were insanely gorgeous guys *ever* nice?

'Because if it is,' she continued, folding her arms, 'Then it's pretty pathetic. I told you that I was sorry for not having paid sufficient attention to the weather, but I left very early this morning so that I could do a little skiing before I went into town and, yes, it was snowing, but nothing like it's snowing now...'

Had she just told him that his apology was pathetic?

'I'm not going to waste time discussing whether you should or shouldn't have been on the slopes in bad weather.'

'*And...*' she carried on, because she wasn't ready to pack in the conversation just yet. They were going to be spending at least another night under the same roof and she might as well clear the air or else they would be circling one another like opponents in a boxing ring, waiting to see who landed the first blow.

'There's more?'

'You had no right to storm into that café and start laying down laws as though you're my lord and master. You're not.'

'I never said I was.'

'I've been taken for a mug by my ex and I haven't come over here for a complete stranger to pick up where he left off!' Okay, so some exaggeration here but, the more Milly thought about her idiocy in actually thinking that Lucas was a nice guy, the angrier she became. She thought of the high-handed, autocratic way he had delivered his command for her to follow him or else find herself stuck trying to get into a hotel—because she wouldn't be able to make it back to the lodge, presumably because *he* would have had no qualms about leaving her to her own devices, having made sure grudgingly that she hadn't died on the slopes…

Lucas was outraged at that suggestion. She had somehow managed to swat aside the small technicality of her rashly having ventured out without due care and attention because she had wanted to have a little 'early-morning ski' before 'dashing to the shops for something and nothing and a cup of hot chocolate'. While he had been worried, imagining her skiing round and round in ever decreasing circles in a wilderness of unfamiliar white, she had been gaily sightseeing! And, when he'd run her to ground, not only had she expected an apology but she had the barefaced nerve to compare him to an ex-fiancé who had made off with her best friend!

Was there a crazier way to join dots?

'So now I'm on a par with a guy who strung you along before he got caught in bed with your best friend?'

'I'm *drawing a comparison*.' Milly pushed herself away from the counter and turned her back on him so that she could make herself a cup of coffee. She could feel his eyes boring into her back. Typical! He was charm personified when she was obeying his rules but the second she so much as expressed an opinion that didn't happen to tally with his, the second she stood up to him and refused to let him treat her like a kid, he suddenly couldn't see her point of view!

'It's a ridiculous comparison and I'm not having this conversation. The phone lines are temporarily dead, and it looks as though I'm going to be staying on here a little longer than I originally anticipated, so you might want to rethink your sulkiness—because it's going to be a little charged if you're either jumping down my throat or stalking around in surly silence.'

Had he actually considered the challenge of bedding the woman? Was there a less appropriate candidate? He shot her a glance of pure exasperation. How much more illogical could one human being be? And how much more temperamental? One minute, she was as chirpy as a cricket, pouring out her life story with gay abandon. The next minute, she was a raging inferno, behaving as though his act of kindness in putting himself out to find her had been *offensive* somehow.

'I just bet you're like that with all those women who fling themselves at your feet,' Milly snapped, turning back to face him and plonking herself at the kitchen table with her mug of coffee in front of her.

'Are we still embroiled in this pointless argument?' Lucas flung his hands in the air and then raked his fingers through his dark hair and folded his arms. 'Like *what*?' He wondered why he was being drawn into this when there was nothing to stop him getting up and walking out of the kitchen, leaving her to stew. 'What am I like with all those women who fling themselves at my feet?'

Histrionic scenes annoyed him. In fact, he could think of nothing more unacceptable than a woman having a hissy fit. Women should be obliging, soothing, a source of undemanding pleasure to interrupt the ferocity and stress of his working life.

He assumed that the only reason he was putting up with the red-faced, throbbing little ruffled angel in front of him was because she wasn't *his* woman.

More to the point, he wasn't exactly awash with choices, considering she was in his lodge, sharing his space.

But you could always walk away, a little voice in his head pointed out, and Lucas brushed it aside. This was not an occasion for walking away.

'High-handed and annoying!'

'You're telling me that you find me *annoying*?'

'You think you can do whatever you like because of the way you look.'

Lucas smiled, a slow, devastating smile that made her pulses jump. 'Is there a backhanded compliment in there somewhere?'

'No. I bet you play the field and lead women on because you *can*...'

Lucas stifled a groan. 'You're like a dog with a bone.'

'I take it there's a backhanded compliment in there somewhere?' Milly parroted tartly and his smile broadened. How was she supposed to get on with the business of being angry with him when he smiled like that? How was she supposed to remember what an arrogant jerk he could be?

Lucas tilted his head to one side, as though seriously considering her rhetorical question.

'Possibly,' he said slowly, his dark eyes roving over

her flushed face. 'I'm surprised you stuck it out in a job where you were forced to take orders.'

Milly glared. It had taken a lot of tongue biting to work in a hot, understaffed kitchen where she had never been given the opportunity actually to produce anything of her own…but she still didn't care for him pointing that out to her.

'There are always up sides to any situation,' he told her, accurately reading the expression on her face and following her thoughts as seamlessly as if they were written in big, bold letters across her forehead. 'You can waste time feeling sorry about yourself and moaning about the job you've lost…'

'I wasn't moaning!'

'Of course you were. Or, you can see it as a good thing. So you no longer have to run around taking orders from someone you don't particularly like in a job that was going nowhere anyway. And, getting back to your sweeping generalisation that I lead women on because *I can,* I think it's wise for me to dispel that myth before it has time to blossom into another full-blown argument.'

His dark eyes were cool and Milly stiffened.

'I'm not interested in—'

'Well you'd better start working up an interest because, frankly, I wasn't interested in hearing you compare me to the bum who let you down.'

Milly reddened because she knew that she had been unfair.

'You were high-handed,' she began weakly in her defence and the temperature in his eyes dropped a few notches from cool to glacial.

'I've already told you that I would never sleep with any woman who was involved with someone else. Likewise, I would never sleep with any woman if *I* was involved with someone else. The thought of that disgusts me, so I couldn't be further from the unprincipled bastard you got yourself involved with.' He didn't take his eyes off her face. 'When I go out with a woman, she is safe in the knowledge that I'm not going anywhere else and I'm not looking anywhere else either.'

Milly shivered at the rampant possessiveness in his voice. She wondered what it would be like to have that possessiveness directed on *her,* to have this big, powerful man focus all his attention on *her,* to the exclusion of anybody else.

'And yet you're not a jealous guy.' She moved on the conversation to dispel the alluring thought of him wanting her so badly that he literally didn't have eyes for any other woman. Her skin tingled, as though he had brushed it with his fingers, and her whole body shrieked into heated response.

'I've never had cause to be.'

'Because all those women who come running when you snap your fingers wouldn't dream of ever giving you anything to be jealous about?' She thought of the way everyone had looked at him in that expensive café, on the street as they'd been leaving...

Something stirred at the back of her mind but she shoved it aside because she wanted to hear what he had to say.

'Because I have yet to meet anyone I'm interested enough in,' Lucas answered bluntly. He picked up his phone, searching for the signal that might or might not appear at any given moment. The lines were down but hopefully not for long. Like anywhere else where the weather could become suddenly and wildly unpredictable, there was no telling when normality would be restored.

The endless cry of the commitment-phobe, Milly thought. Men who could have whoever they wanted never had an interest in settling for one because why opt for one type of candy when there were so many jars and bottles to choose from? He could barely be bothered to have this conversation with her. He was searching his phone for a signal. She knew that. He was desperate for an outside line and connection with the real world. He'd already gone beyond the line of duty in putting himself out to stage a rescue mission for someone he happened to be stuck with.

'Am I boring you?' she asked and Lucas looked at her.

'You're the most demanding woman I have ever met in my entire life.'

'What's that supposed to mean?' Milly bristled.

'You're still annoyed because I rescued you?' Lucas had never done so much delving into any woman's psyche in his life before. Even in his wild and misspent youth, when he had been gunning for the wrong woman, he had let sex do the talking.

'Don't start thinking of yourself as a knight in shining armour,' Milly jumped in to correct him and he raised his eyebrows in an expression that was lazy and amused.

'Ah. Still annoyed. Where has Little Miss Sunshine gone?'

In a flash, Milly had insight into what he thought of her. While she had been shooting her mouth off, *confiding,* losing herself in the thrill of being in the company of a guy who was actually *listening* to her...not to mention thrilling her with those dark, saturnine good looks…he had not been similarly entranced. The opposite. She had been a spot of comic relief with her 'Little Miss Sunshine' personality.

She turned away, hurt.

'I apologise if you were embarrassed,' he said gruffly. 'I realise that, along with *arrogant,* I can be prone to occasionally lapsing into caveman tactics.' When she didn't say anything, he reached forward and, finger on her chin, turned her gently to face him.

Milly's eyes widened and her body was suddenly, horrifyingly, excitingly, in meltdown. She could barely breathe. Her mouth parted. Her nipples stiffened, poking against her bra, sensitive as they scraped against the cotton. Between her legs, she was dampening.

'Hell, you should be careful when you look at a man like that,' Lucas said roughly. But he didn't remove his finger. His libido had been in retreat for a while. Dealing with his ex had left a sour taste in his mouth and he had submerged himself in work because it was, frankly, blessed relief from the whining demands of a woman who didn't want to go away.

Milly, with her disingenuous ignorance of who he really was, with her open, confiding nature and her easy laughter—despite having come through circumstances that would have knocked back anyone else— had stirred his interest.

'Forget it. Not interested.' She pulled away and stood up. 'Just out of curiosity, when were you thinking of leaving?'

Lucas felt the reassuring buzz of his mobile as the outside world was once more connected. Normality could be restored within twenty-four hours. This unusual interlude could be left where it was and he could return to his formidably controlled and predictable life.

Since when had he ever been a fan of surprises anyway? Since when had he ever been interested in exploring anything that came in an unpredictable package? Hadn't he already been there? Done that? Got burned?

'I'm considering my options.'

'That being the case, I suggest we do our own thing. If I decide to go out skiing, then I don't expect you to instigate a search party if I happen to be a couple of hours late.'

Lucas shook his head and briefly closed his eyes. 'Demanding,' he drawled. 'And bloody stubborn.'

'Would that be because I disapproved of you making an idiot out of me in a public place?' She opened her mouth to fume a little bit more but his phone beeped with a series of incoming text messages, voicemails and emails.

Exasperated, she walked off towards the window where the furious snowfall was already showing signs of abating. Blue sky was doing its best to break through. By tomorrow, if not later in the day, the skiing would be good.

And who knew? Lucas might be gone.

She told herself that that would be the best possible outcome. She needed her time out, undiluted time to mourn the passing of a significant relationship. Under normal circumstances, if the Ramos family had showed up, she would have been busy but her busyness would not have distracted her from her thoughts. Lucas distracted her from her thoughts. Robbie had barely registered on her radar! In fact, when she tried to think of him, a darker, leaner image instantly superimposed itself.

Behind her, she was aware of Lucas talking rapidly on his phone. He seemed to be very well known in these parts. A man with connections. He was probably doing all sorts of networking right now, getting things lined up now that his stint here had fallen through.

'You were asking me,' a dark, sexy drawl said from behind her, 'how long I intended staying here and I told you that I was keeping my options open...'

Milly spun around, tensing up. 'I'm fine to stay here by myself,' she told him without hesitation.

'But would that require you to curb your keen sense of adventure?' Lucas couldn't help asking. He thought of her here, on her own, deciding to explore the slopes at midnight just for the fun of it. 'Tell me what your plans are when you leave this place. Do you intend to stay here for the full fortnight? Or will you return to London and start looking for another flatmate? What happens if you don't find one? '

Milly frowned, taken aback at his change of subject. 'I'm keeping my options open,' she mimicked, and Lucas smiled.

'Come and sit down. I want to have a talk with you.'

'What about?'

Lucas didn't answer. Instead, he strolled towards the sofa, his face revealing nothing of what was going through his head.

Was there anything more annoying than an actively functioning grapevine? He had been in the town no longer than an hour and the world at large seemed to know.

His window of freedom appeared to have shut and now he had a problem on his hands.

Of course, there was no problem that did not carry a solution, but he could definitely have done without this particular thorn in his side. His mouth tightened as he thought of the series of texts he had received, texts that had been in a toxic holding bay until service resumed and he could pick them up.

'What are the chances of you finding a job the second you return to London?' he asked, relaxing back on the sofa, his face revealing nothing of what was going through his head or of the vague plan slowly beginning to cohere into shape. 'In the catering arena? I'm guessing that there are a lot of jobs to work at burger joints but I'm also guessing that those jobs won't be top of your list.'

'I honestly don't see what my future job hunting has to do with you!'

'And then there's the little technicality of paying rent when you don't have a job. Difficult. Unless you have a stash of money saved...' He steamrollered over her interruption as though she hadn't spoken. 'Have you a stash of money saved?'

'That's none of your—'

'Business. Is that what you're about to say?'

'Where are you going with this, Lucas? Okay, so I may not have much money saved, but...I'll have what I've earned for this fortnight.' She frowned and wondered how long that would last. Why did he have to throw reality in her face? Had he no heart *at all*?

'"Water through fingers" is the thought that springs to mind,' Lucas said with what she thought was a callous lack of empathy. 'The cost of living is astronomical in London.'

'How would you know?' Milly muttered and again Lucas opted to ignore her interruption.

'I guess, in all events, you could always return to your grandmother's place in Scotland. Ah. I can see from the you way you blanched just then that that option lacks appeal.'

'Why are you doing this?'

'Doing what?' Lucas asked with a show of innocence that set her teeth on edge because it was so clearly false.

'Ramming all my problems down my throat. I wish I'd never confided in you.'

'I wasn't ramming your problems down your throat.'

'I didn't come here to…to…'

'Confront that awkward little thing known as *reality*?'

'You can be really horrible.' Okay, so obviously she would have to address the pressing issue of how she was going to survive without a job and, hard on the heels of that, probably nowhere to live either. But she had been quite happy to put that on hold, at least for a few days. Once she had sorted out the emotional mess she was in which, thinking about it, she realised she seemed to be sorting out rather nicely, all things taken into account.

'There's a point to my timely reminder of the problems you're facing,.' Lucas leaned forward, resting his forearms on his thighs. He wondered where he should start. Her mouth was pursed into a sulky downturn, her eternally upbeat personality dampened by the way he had forced unpleasant reality upon her.

'And that point being…?'

'Point being that I'm about to come to your rescue. In fact, I'm about to open up your world to tantalising new possibilities, and in return all you have to do for me is one small favour.'

CHAPTER FIVE

MILLY STARED AT Lucas in confusion. For a few seconds, she wondered whether he was joking, whether he was having a laugh at her expense, somehow getting his own back for the tantrum she had pulled earlier.

She dismissed that idea as fast as it had come. His face was impassive, deadly serious. And if her gut was telling her that he wasn't the sort of guy who liked tantrums, it was also telling her that he wasn't the sort of guy who would do anything to get his own back for something as silly as her snapping at him.

Whether he had deserved it or not. Which he had. More or less.

'Tantalising new possibilities?' she laughed a little weakly. 'Are you feeling okay, Lucas? How are you going to open up my world to *tantalising new possibilities*?' She wished he would stop looking at her like that, with such deadly calm.

'You might be a little…surprised by what I'm about to tell you.'

'Then don't tell me,' she said promptly. 'I hate surprises. They're never good.'

'Well, that's one thing we have in common,' Lucas murmured, momentarily distracted. He stood up and she followed the easy, fluid movement of his long body

with something close to compulsion. He walked across
to the window and stared out and, even with his back to
her, she could tell that he wasn't really seeing what he
appeared to be staring at. She could sense his distraction and that made her nervous because, and she could
see this now, there was something so intensely *focused*
about him. *Distracted* was not his normal frame of mind.

He spun round, caught her staring at him and allowed himself a small smile which immediately made
her glower. And *that* was why he was just so damned
arrogant, she thought. Because women followed him
with their eyes, irresistibly drawn to mindless gazing.

'I'm not quite the person you think I am.'

For a few seconds, Milly thought that perhaps she
had misheard him. Who on earth ever said stuff like
that? Her mouth fell open and she stared at him in silence, waiting for him to enlarge on that enigmatic
statement.

Lucas was taking his time. He walked slowly back
towards her, maintaining eye contact.

'And, before your over-active imagination starts cast-
ing me in the starring role of homicidal maniac, you
can rest assured that it's nothing like that.' He sat down
and continued looking at her thoughtfully, trying on
the various options at his disposal for telling her who
he really was and what he wanted from her. And why.
Much as he loathed justifying his decisions to anyone,
he would have no choice in this circumstance.

'The Ramos family,' he began. 'This house…every-
thing in it…doesn't belong to them.'

'Oh, please…' Milly raised her eyebrows in rampant disbelief. 'I don't know where you're going with
this but I know for a fact that it does. You forget that
snooty Sandra employed me to work for them. I was

given all their details. Are you going to tell me that she made the whole thing up? That there are no such people? Plus, you're forgetting that Mr Ramos paid me for my time here!'

She shot him a look of triumph at winning this argument, mixed with pity that he had chosen to come out with such a glaring lie. The combination felt good, especially after the way he had hauled her out of the café in front of everyone. Triumph and pity…she savoured the feeling for a few seconds and threw in a kindly but condescending smile for good measure.

Lucas, she noted, didn't come close to looking sheepish.

'Of course he paid you,' he said, brushing aside that detail as casually as someone brushing aside a piffling point of view that carried no weight. 'He paid you because I told him to.'

'Because you told him to…' Milly burst out laughing and, when eventually her laughter had turned to broken giggles, she carried on, very gently, 'I think you might be delusional. I know you fancy yourself as some kind of hot shot just because you happen to work for loads of rich people and you probably have them eating out of your hand…' *Especially the women.* 'But the bottom line is that you're still just a ski instructor'

Lucas kissed sweet, rueful goodbye to his very brief window of normality.

'Not quite…'

'I mean,' Milly expanded, ignoring him, 'it's a bit like me saying that I own five Michelin-starred restaurants when in fact I just happen to work behind the scenes for an average hotel in West London.'

'Worked,' Lucas swiftly reminded her and she scowled at the reminder. 'You *worked* at an average

hotel in West London. Don't forget that you're now jobless.'

'I hadn't forgotten,' Milly said through gritted teeth. 'And I still don't know where you're going with this.'

Lucas sighed and raked his fingers through his hair, then he reached for his computer, which was on the glass table next to him.

With a start of surprise he realised that for the first time in a very long time indeed work had not been the overriding thought in his head. In fact, he had a back-log of emails to work his way through, emails to which he had given precious little thought. Dark eyes lazily took in the diminutive girl in front of him sitting in a lotus position, her long hair flowing in rivulets over her shoulders. Self-restraint with a sexy member of the opposite sex had clearly had an effect on his ability to concentrate to his usual formidably high levels.

He kick-started the computer and when he had found what he had been looking for he swivelled the computer towards her.

Milly looked at him sceptically. Did anything faze this guy? Whatever the situation, he was the very picture of cool. Chewing her out in the middle of an expensive café in one of the most expensive ski resorts on the planet: *cool.* Arranging for her to stay in the ski lodge: *cool.* Telling her a string of real whoppers about the extent of his influence: *cool.*

'You're not meant to carry on sitting there,' Lucas informed her gently. 'You're meant to get close enough to the computer so that you can actually read what I've flagged up.'

Accustomed to having the world jump to his commands without asking questions, Lucas had a brief moment of wondering whether she intended stubbornly to stay put until he was forced to bring the computer to her. However, after a few seconds of jaundiced hesitation, Milly stood up and then sat on the sofa, back in her cross-legged position, so that she could read his extensive bio.

Lucas watched her. She didn't have to say anything; her face said it all: calm and superior, morphing into frowning puzzlement, then finally incredulity.

Then she did it all over again as she re-read the article, which, fawningly and in depth, traced his lineage and every single one of his achievements, from university degrees to acquisitions of companies. Much was made of his background and the limitless privileges into which he had been born.

He had been personally interviewed for this article. It had come hard on the heels of his unfortunate experience with his gold-digging almost-fiancée, and he had not been predisposed to be anything but brusque with the glamorous blonde whose job it had been to glean some scintillating 'heard it from the horse's mouth' tit-bits.

His coolness had not bothered her. She had practically salivated in his company and had crossed and re-crossed her long legs so many times that he had asked her at one point whether she needed to use the toilet.

At any rate, the finished article had been sent to him for proofreading before it had been put online, and he had been amused to note that he had somehow achieved a god-like status, even though he knew he had been borderline rude to the woman. Money: Was there anything in the world that talked louder and more persuasively?

'I don't understand.' Milly sat back, drawing her legs up and looping her arms around them.

'Of course you do.'

'Don't tell me what I do or don't understand,' she said automatically, because there was nothing worse than an arrogant know-it-all. But he was right. She understood. 'You're not a ski instructor at all, are you?'

'Correct.'

'In other words, you lied to me.'

'I wouldn't exactly call it a lie…' Naturally he had expected surprise, incredulity even, but at the end of the day the ski instructor had been swapped for a billionaire. He had taken it as a given that his new status would do its usual job and bring a smile of servile appreciation to her lips. None of it. She was scowling at him, eyes glinting with anger.

'Well, *I* would.' Milly was struggling to contain her anger. How dared he? How dared he play her for a complete fool? But then, she was just Little Miss Sunshine, wasn't she? Some comic relief for a man marooned in a ski lodge with her!

'You made false assumptions,' Lucas told her with barely concealed impatience. 'I chose not to set you straight.'

'In your world, that might be acceptable behaviour. In my world, that's called lying!' She sprang to her feet and stormed over to the window, stared out for a little while and then stormed back towards him, hands on her hips. 'I leave London to escape a creep who lied to me and what do I land up sharing space with? Another creep who lies to me!'

'That's the last time you're going to insult me by bracketing me with your loser ex!'

'Why? You seem to have a fair few things in common! Why didn't you just tell me who you were?'

Because I was enjoying the novelty of being with someone refreshingly honest… Because in a world

*where wariness and suspicion are bywords, it was a
holiday not having to guard every syllable, watch every
turn of phrase, accept instant adulation without being
able really to distinguish what was genuine and what
was promoted by a healthy knowledge of how much I
was worth...*

'When you're as rich as I am, it pays to be careful.'

'In other words, I could have been just another cheap,
tacky gold-digger after your money!'

'If you want to put it like that...'

His dark eyes were cool, assessing, unflinching. She
could have hit him. How could he just *sit there* and
admit to lying to her without even batting an eyelid?
As though it was just perfectly acceptable?

Although...

The man was a billionaire. He owned a million companies. He had a hand in pretty much every pie and
he had come from money. There were no limits to his
wealth, his power, his influence, it would seem. She
could reluctantly understand that suspicion would be
his constant companion.

That thought instantly deflated her and she had to
summon up some of the old anger she had felt at the
thought that he had cheerfully lied to her.

'I feel sorry for you,' she told him scornfully and
he stiffened.

'Do I really want to hear you explain that remark?'
No one, but no one, had ever felt sorry for him or, if
anyone had, they had been at pains to conceal it. Money
engendered quite the opposite response. Money combined with good looks—which was something about
himself he accepted without any vanity whatsoever—
was even more persuasive a tool in affording him the

sort of slavish responses he got from other people. Particularly from women.

He looked at her carefully. She was as volatile and as unpredictable as a volcano on the point of eruption. It should have been a turn off and it was mildly surprising that it wasn't.

'How can you trust that anyone likes you for you?'

'My point exactly. But, before we deviate down some amateur psychobabble road, there's a reason I have brought this up.'

Milly stilled. There would be a reason, of course there would, or else he would have stayed a couple of nights and pushed on leaving her none the wiser. Certainly he would have spared himself the sort of awkward conversation he clearly wasn't relishing.

But before he got to that… She finally grasped the thought that had been niggling away at the back of her mind.

'At that café,' she said slowly, 'The owner… I wondered why he was so eager to please…why he said that I didn't have to pay the bill.'

'I'm known here.' He offered an elegant shrug. 'I don't come often but when I do I'm high-profile.'

High-profile and made of money. What had he thought of her? Babbling on and taking him for being a ski instructor? He must have thought that she was crazy. A crazy woman who chattered non-stop and had ruined his seclusion by landing on his doorstep.

'Why did you decide to come over?' she asked, feverishly pursuing her train of thought so that she could join the pieces of the puzzle together and get the complete picture.

Lucas hesitated. It was for the very reason that he had decided to descend on his ski lodge that he was now having this conversation. 'Everyone needs a break,' he informed her silkily. 'Alberto and his annoying family had pulled out and I decided that a bit of skiing would be just the thing. And, in case you're wondering, the Ramos family were over here as a favour to my mother. Alberto works for me.'

'Which was why you could engineer to have me paid for this this two-week holiday. You just had to pick the phone up and tell him and he had to obey. Is that what happens in your life, Lucas? You snap your fingers and people jump to attention and obey you?'

'In a nutshell.'

Milly wondered how she hadn't noticed before the way that he was sheathed in an invisible aura of power, the sort of power that only the super-rich had. Or maybe she *had* noticed but, in her usual trusting way, had shoved that to the back of her mind and chosen to take him at his word: Mr Ski Instructor who did a bit of *this and that* when he wasn't teaching people like the Ramos family to ski.

Maybe, just maybe, she would wake up one day and realise that people were rarely who they said they were.

'Sit down, Milly.' He waited until she was back on the sofa. Her eyes were guarded, the cheerful smile wiped off her face. He had done that. Whatever he told her, he would be just someone else who had lied to her. His mouth tightened; for once, he was finding it hard casually to dismiss someone else's emotions. Habits of lifetime, however, came to his rescue and he swept past his temporary discomfort. So he had punctured some of that bubbly sparkle. Cynicism was healthy. It prepared you for life's adversities. She would return to this very point in time and, in the years to come, she would thank him for bursting her bubble.

'I told you that I came here because I needed a break. Partially true. I'm responsible for the running of...countless companies that stretch across countless countries. I employ thousands...and I'm responsible for them, as well.'

So many revelations were piling up that she felt faint. He was a one-man employment agency. He was a guy who ruled the world, someone who dropped in now and again for a bit of skiing when he needed to unwind, someone who had the most amazing ski lodge on the planet, which he used for a few days in the year. She would stake her life on him having a house in every country, places like the ski lodge that he could use when and if it suited him.

'What do you mean when you say *partially*? You said that it was *partially true* that you came here to unwind. What other reason would you have for coming here?'

'I have been experiencing a few problems with an ex,' Lucas said heavily. Unaccustomed as he was to accounting for his actions, he was decidedly ill at ease with explaining himself to the woman sitting opposite him, but explain himself he had to.

'No, let me guess.' Milly's voice was a shade higher than normal. The whole situation felt surreal. In fact, the past few *weeks* had felt surreal. *You'd think I'd be used to dealing with surreal by now,* she thought with an edge of bitterness that was alien to her. 'The ex wasn't ready to be an ex. Did the poor woman start getting ideas about settling down with you?'

Lucas found it difficult to think of Isobel in terms of 'the poor woman'. She was anything *but* a helpless, deluded damsel with a broken heart. She was a sophisticated, hard-as-nails, six-foot model who had capitalised on the fact that, very slightly, she was acquainted with his mother. She had mistakenly figured that the connection carried weight. His parents had known her parents, both wealthy families living in Madrid, both mixing in the same social circles. The relationship had fizzled out when his father had died but she had done her utmost to resuscitate it during their six-month fling in the hope that familiarity would somehow guide him to a flashbulb moment of thinking that what they had was more than what it actually was. It hadn't but she still refused to let go.

'My relationship with Isobel was not of the enduring kind.'

'Don't you *ever* want to settle down? What was she like? Why wasn't it of the enduring kind?' Curiosity dug into her. 'Was she a gold-digger?' She pictured a kid who was too naive to comprehend all the things Lucas *did* and *didn't* do.

'I am a meal ticket for most women,' Lucas responded drily, not flinching from the absolute truth. 'Even for rich women who can manage quite happily on their trust funds. I have a lot of pull, a lot of connections. I offer a lifestyle that most women would find irresistible.'

'What sort of lifestyle is that?'

'What can I say, Milly? I have a passport to places only available to the rich and famous. It's not just about the limitless spending and the shopping sprees, it's also about the mixing and mingling with famous faces and people who appear in magazines.'

'It sounds hideous.'

'You don't mean that.'

'Being on show every minute of the day and living your life in a glass house with everybody looking in? Having to dress up for social affairs every night?

Wear war-paint and make sure you're shopping in all the right places and mixing with all the right people, even if they're dull and shallow and boring? I'd hate it.'

Which was why she had been such a breath of fresh air—enough of a breath of fresh air to make him alter his plans for leaving. Anonymity had brought him a glimpse of being the sort of man who could dump his cynicism for a minute...except cynicism was just much too ingrained in him for him ever really to do that. And besides, that glimpse of freedom was now gone.

Lucas gazed at her open, honest face and wondered whether she would be singing the same song if she were to be introduced to that life of glamour and wealth that she claimed she would hate. It was very easy to dismiss the things you've never personally experienced.

'All this is by the by,' he said with a shrug. 'The fact is that Isobel has been annoyingly persistent in thinking that we can salvage something and carry on. She's refused to fade away and, having finally reconciled herself to the end of our relationship, she's decided that a little healthy revenge might be called for. When I went looking for you in the town, I was snapped.'

'Snapped?'

'Surely you can't be *that* naive, Milly. The paparazzi are always on the lookout for candid shots of high-profile people. In fairness, I don't know whether I was snapped by the paparazzi or by some interested visitor who recognised me. Or maybe Alberto's wife just happened to let slip to someone who let slip to someone else that I was staying at the lodge with you... Whatever picture happened to be taken of us together consolidated the story. I would think that someone who knows Isobel posted it to her on a social network and it went from there…'

'Sorry, but you're losing me. What story? There *is* no story. Not unless it's the story of the ski instructor who wasn't a ski instructor.'

'Are we back to that?'

'Tell me what you're talking about,' Milly said because he was right. What was there to gain from going over trodden ground? So he had lied because he was suspicious of the human race and in particular of women. She could tell him a thousand times that she found it insulting and offensive but he would just look at her blandly, shrug and imply that her point of view was inferior to his.

'Isobel has somehow managed to get hold of the fact that I'm here with you.'

'You're not here *with me*.' She flushed hotly at the unspoken implication buzzing in the air between them like a live, dangerous electric current.

'And I'm perfectly sure,' Lucas intoned in a voice that was suddenly hard and devoid of emotion, 'that she is all too aware of that. But she's a woman scorned and she's decided that a little malicious mischief is just what I deserve. She can't have me so why not make life as hellish for me as she can, to teach me the valuable lesson that, when it comes to dumping, she's the one who decides to do it?'

Milly frowned in confusion. For someone who had an exceptional grasp of the English language and how to use it to maximum benefit, he seemed to be struggling with his words. 'Okay…' She dragged out that one word while trying to grapple with whatever he was attempting to say to her.

'There's something else I should mention,' Lucas

admitted. 'Another reason I came here was to have a break from my mother. She's been ill and, ever since her extremely successful operation, she's managed to convince herself that time is no longer on her side...'

'I'm sorry. Happens with older people sometimes,' Milly murmured. 'My granny had an operation on her hip two years ago and, even though she can run up a mountain faster than a goat, she still thinks that she'll wake up one morning and she won't be able to stand. Sorry. I interrupted you. What does your mother have to do with this? Lucas, I haven't got the foggiest what you're talking about.'

'Isobel,' he said heavily, striving to stem the anger in his voice when he thought of where his ex had landed him, 'has presented my mother with whatever picture was snapped of us in town and has intimated that...' he shook his head and cursed fluently under his breath '...we are somehow involved in some kind of romantic situation.'

He flushed darkly, remembering the way his libido had gone into orbit when he had looked at her. Yes, he had toyed with the tantalising thought of taking her to his bed. Had that thought somehow manifested itself in whatever expression he had been snapped wearing? Had he been looking at her with some kind of sexual intent? Had some idiot's camera caught him off-guard with a look in his eye that had lent itself to some kind of misinterpretation?

Milly's mouth fell open. She didn't know whether to be horrified, incredulous or just downright amused. No. Not amused. His expression was grim. If she laughed, then he wouldn't be laughing along with her.

'But that's ridiculous.' *Who in their right mind would link the two of us together romantically?* 'I've been here for a couple of days. How on earth would anyone suppose that we're somehow *romantically linked*?' She tried a laugh of sorts and, as expected, he saw nothing funny in the situation. 'Besides, I'm here recovering from a broken heart. Don't forget I was due to be married less than a month ago...'

'She's implied to my mother that we may have known one another longer than a mere couple of days. She knows how I feel about involvement and permanence because I told her, and she knows that the last thing I would want is to find myself trapped in a situation where my mother thinks that I may have ditched my bachelor ways...'

'How do you feel about involvement and permanence?'

'Another time, Milly. For now, you just need to know that they don't form part of my lifestyle choices.'

Milly burst out laughing. 'I just can't picture it!' She gasped. 'I just can't imagine you sneaking around my miniscule two-bed house, comforting me after my break-up. Somehow I don't think you're the kind of guy to go unnoticed! And then what? We planned a secret rendezvous here via snooty Sandra and her band of clones? It doesn't add up. Any fool would be able to see through that in seconds!' She sobered up. 'But that was a mean trick. I guess she fell in love with you. Poor woman.'

Lucas raised his eyebrows, momentarily disconcerted. If he hadn't had proof positive that Milly wasn't interested in what he brought to the table, he would have put her down as just another gold-digger with a slightly different approach. 'I'll cut to the chase,' he said tightly. 'She's told my mother that we're slightly more than an item. My mother is now under the impression that we're going to be married. Isobel showed her whatever candid snapshot got taken and presented her case as the utter truth because would I have gone for someone so…different from what I usually go for if it weren't for the fact that we were serious about one another?'

'What do you usually go for?' She mentally answered that question for herself before she had finished asking it. The guy was drop-dead gorgeous and rolling in money as an added bonus. Guys like that only went for a certain type and that type wasn't *her*. 'No, don't answer that,' she told him quietly. 'I'm thinking you like lots of supermodel types, stunning arm-candy. I'll bet your jilted Isobel was tall and skinny and looked like a model.'

'She *was* a model.'

'So she's pulled a pretty clever trick in showing your mum a picture of dumpy little me, because why else would you be in the same *room* as me unless it was serious. Am I right?'

'That's more or less the size of it. She must have glossed over the holes in the story and ran amok with the rest because my mother's fallen for whatever she's been told hook, line and unfortunate sinker.'

'Do you know what, Lucas?' She breathed in deeply and marvelled at how complicated her life had become ever since Robbie had entered it—lying, cheating Robbie who had come along and wreaked havoc with her perfectly enjoyable, uneventful, contented life. And, not satisfied with that, fate had decided to carry on where Robbie had left off and had thrown her a blinder in the form of the man now looking at her with dark, lazy intent.

'I think I need a break from the male species. In fact, I might take a permanent break from them. Anyway, I don't know why you've told me all this. I'm sorry your mother now thinks that you've found the love of your life but you'll just have to tell her the truth.'

'There is an alternative...' He stood and flexed his arms, stretching out from having sat in one spot for too long when he had wanted to move around, walk some of his restlessness away.

'Which is what, exactly...?' Milly looked at him cautiously as he prowled through the vast open space. *His* vast open space. She still found it hard to grapple with the reality that all of this belonged to *him*. That said, she had recognised a certain something the very first time she had met him: a certain air that spoke of power; a certain arrogant self-assurance that made a nonsense of him being someone as relatively unimportant as a ski instructor. Even a drop-dead, improbably gorgeous ski instructor.

Another telling example of her stupid ability to trust even when she was staring evidence to the contrary in the face.

'You're broke, you're out of work and you'll probably return to London to find all your possessions tossed onto the pavement, awaiting your urgent collection.'

'My landlord wouldn't do that,' Milly said coldly. 'Tenants *do* have rights, you know.'

'Not as many as a landlord whose primary right is the one to have his rent paid.' He paused to stare down at her and Milly grudgingly gazed back up at him. 'Here's the deal. I employ you for a couple of weeks—three, max—to play the role of loved-up wife-to-be. We will stay with my mother in her house in the outskirts of Madrid, a beautiful city by the way, and we can break up over there. My mother will be saddened but she will recover. Normally, I wouldn't go to this much trouble but, like I said, she's been ill and she's mentally not quite there yet. I don't want to present her with a litany of low tricks and lies. She will be upset and confused, especially coming hard on the heels of wanting me to settle down. I will give her what she wants and, when she sees how impossible I am, she will understand why marriage is off the cards for me for the foreseeable future.

'And here's what you get out of this: a fat pay cheque, a five-star, all expenses paid holiday in Spain and, afterwards, I will ensure that you're set up with a damn good job in one of the three restaurants I own in London, with full use of one of my company apartments for six months until you can find alternative accommodation to rent. Whatever you were earning in your last job… Put it this way, I'll quadruple the package.'

'And in return I lie to your mother.'

'That's not how I see it.'

'Plus I lie to my grandmother as well, I suppose? Because what am I supposed to tell her when I don't return to London? Plus I lie to my friends, as well? Thanks, Lucas, but no thanks…'

CHAPTER SIX

So why was she now, a mere day and a half later, sitting in splendid luxury on a private plane heading to Salamanca on the outskirts of Madrid?

Next to her, Lucas was absorbed in a bewildering array of figures on the computer screen blinking in front of him. The 'this and that' had kept billionaires busy and hard at it.

Milly sighed. She knew why she was here; she was just too soft-natured. It was an emotional hazard that was close cousin to the 'overly trusting' side of her that had propelled her into naively believing that the billionaire with the private jet had been a ski instructor—which in turn had been the same side of her that had encouraged her to think that Robbie the cheat had been in love with her rather than mildly fond and willing to exploit.

'You're sighing. Tell me that you haven't done a U-turn on your decision.' Lucas snapped shut his computer and sprawled back in the oversized seat, which was just one of the many perks of having his own plane— no unwelcome strangers crowding his personal space and as much leg room as he needed. He was a big man.

He looked at her, his dark eyes lazily drifting over the baby-smooth, soft curves of her open, expressive face. She had tied her long hair back but, as usual, unruly curls were refusing to be flattened into obedience.

'What would you do if I told you that I had? We're in mid-air. Would you chuck me out of your plane? I still can't believe that you actually *own this,* Lucas.'

'I don't employ strong-arm tactics, Milly. So no, in answer to your question, I wouldn't chuck you out of the plane. And I'm getting a little tired of hearing you tell me how incredulous you find it that I happen to be rich.'

'You can't blame me. I don't meet many people who own ski lodges and private planes.' Her voice bore the lingering remnants of accusation.

'I suppose I should be grateful that you're no longer lecturing me for being a lying bastard like your long-gone ex-fiancé. Why are you sighing? If we're going to do a passable imitation of being a loved-up couple, heavy, troubled sighs aren't going to sell it.'

In response, Milly released another sigh as she absently looked at the stunningly beautiful face gazing at her with just the slightest hint of impatience.

'You never told me why you're so averse to settling down.'

'You're right. I didn't.'

'Why not? I've told you loads of stuff. The least you could do is fill me in, or am I supposed to be the clueless girlfriend?'

Lucas raked his fingers through his hair and stared at her in silence for a few seconds. 'I don't confide.'

'And I don't pretend to be someone I'm not.'

'Bloody stubborn,' he muttered under his breath. 'Okay, if you really want to know, I had a poor experience when I was young. Take one pretty girl, making me so out of my normal comfort zone that I didn't think twice about believing the clap trap she concocted, add a phoney pregnancy threat and I give you the sort of gold-digging experience that's made me realise that, when it comes to permanence, the only kind I will ever go for is of the business arrangement variety. I'm a fast learner when it comes to mistakes and never making them again.'

'That's awful,' Milly said, appalled. 'How old were you?'

'This isn't a continuing discussion, Milly.'

'But how old?'

Lucas shook his head, exasperated. 'Nineteen.'

'So you had a bad experience when you were a teenager and you've let it ruin your adult life and all the choices you make?'

'*Ruin?* Wrong word. I prefer *affect*. Like I said, I learn from my mistakes.'

And he wasn't about to budge. She could see that in his eyes and in the grim seriousness of his expression. It chilled her to the bone.

'But what if you one day fall in love?'

'Not on the cards. And, Milly, let's put this conversation to rest now.'

'I never thought that large scale lying was on the cards for *me,* yet here I am…' She rested back and stared off at nothing in particular.

Lying was just not part of her nature and ye here she was, immersed in the biggest lie of her life, and all because she had had a vivid image of his mother, frail, vulnerable, bitterly saddened and disappointed at having to be told that she was the victim of a lying ex-girlfriend. She knew first-hand how much lies could wound. She also knew that men could be utterly blind when it came to health issues. If someone had been recently mown down by a bus and, when asked how they were, replied, 'just fine,' the average man would be in-souciantly inclined to accept the answer at face value.

The average man would also be highly likely to un-derestimate the impact of disappointment on a sick and elderly person. Who knew how Antonia, Lucas's mother, would react if she discovered the depth of the lies told to her? Stress killed. Everyone knew that. Whereas, if she were to see for herself just how un-suited Lucas was to her, Milly, then the termination of their so-called relationship would be no big deal. And unsuitable they most certainly were, especially after what he had just told her…

And, face it, there were all those other perks that would certainly make the horror story called her pres-ent situation so much easier to bear: job secured, ac-commodation secured, no nasty landlord banging on her door demanding to know when his rent would be paid.

She would be able to put her grandmother's mind at ease that her life was back to normal and *it would be*.

'I guess your mother was disappointed that you weren't prepared to tie the knot with your girlfriend. I guess she doesn't know about your hang-ups.' She turned to him, wanting to hear just a little more about her competition, because now that they were en route to unchartered territory she could feel butterflies be-ginning to take up residence in her tummy.

'My hang-ups. You really have a way with words. You conversationally go where no other woman has gone before. My mother may want me to settle down,' he said drily, 'But even she sussed that Isobel wasn't going to be the perfect candidate for the position of stay-at-home wife.'

'Because…?'

'Because Isobel was more jet-setter than home-

maker. I think it goes with the territory of being a supermodel. Something about being treated like a goddess
when, in fact, you're no more than a pretty face.'

'Jet-setter…'

'Glitz, glamour and an unnatural love of having cam-
eras focused on her.'

'The sort of girl you tend to go out with.'

'Why the hundred and one questions, Milly?'

'Because I'm nervous,' she confessed. The way he
described his ex was a fine example of a man who at-
tached himself to just the sort of woman he was in
no danger of wanting to commit to. Casual sex. She
shouldn't even bother to speculate on his motivations
or lack of motivations when it came to women.

'Think of the wonderful payback and your nerves
will disappear. Trust me.'

Milly scowled because, however wonderful those
paybacks were, they weren't the reason she had agreed
to engage in this little game of fiction and, the closer
the plane got to their destination, the more she wondered whether her impulse to do what had felt right at
the time really was such a clever idea.

Her impulses *had* been known to let her down.

'I didn't agree because of the…paybacks.'

Lucas's eyebrows shot up and he gave her a slow,
disbelieving smile.

'You're so suspicious,' Milly muttered.

'You're telling me that your sole reason for agree-
ing to pretend to be my soon-to-be-departed fiancée is
because you felt sorry for my mother, a woman you've
never met in your life?'

'Mostly. Yes.'

'Nice word, *mostly*. Open to all sorts of conflicting
interpretations.'

'Sometimes you really annoy me, Lucas.' Right now he was doing rather more than annoying her. Right now she wished that he would return to his obsessive contemplation of whatever high-powered deal he was in the middle of making, because his attention on her was making her feel all hot and bothered.

Having travelled with nothing suitable to wear for warmer temperatures, she was in a thermal T-shirt, jeans, her thick socks and trainers and the whole ensemble made her skin itch.

'I'm just trying to… Wondering how…to pretend to be someone I'm not.'

'You mean how to pretend to be someone in a relationship with me?'

'I've never done anything like this before. I'm not the sort of girl who likes fooling people. It doesn't seem kind and, whether you want to believe me or not, yes, the paybacks will certainly make my life a whole lot easier when I get back to London but mostly I'm doing this because I hate thinking that your mother's had her hopes raised only to have them dashed, and cruelly dashed at that. I honestly can't believe that anyone could tell such a horrendous lie to someone who hasn't been well, just to get revenge because you let her down.

'Has your mother *ever* been keen on *any* of your girlfriends?'

'Not that I can recall offhand…' And that had never bothered him until she began making noises about wanting him to settle down because 'who knew what lay round the corner for her?'.

He knew what she thought of the Isobels of his life, the never-ending stream of decorative supermodels who enjoyed basking in his reflective glow; who simpered, acquiesced and tailored themselves to his needs. He, personally, had no problem with any of those traits; his work life was high-powered and stressed enough without adding more stress to the tally in the form of a demanding girlfriend. His mother, always grounded, was of a different opinion.

It occurred to him that this little game of make-believe might have an unexpected benefit.

Milly was as normal and as natural as the day was long. Were it not for his inherently suspicious nature, he would truly believe that, as she had stated, she had agreed to this well-intentioned charade from the goodness of her heart. She was just the sort of wholesome girl he would never seriously consider as a life partner in a million years. No; like it or not, if and when he decided to tie the knot, it would be with someone who saw marriage through the same eyes as his. It would be with someone who didn't need his money, someone who understood the frailty of the institution and recognised, as he did, that marriage stood a far better chance of success if it was approached as a business proposition.

If his mother saw for himself just how unsuited he was for a girl like Milly—and for Milly read all women like her—not only would she accept it when they 'broke up' but she would understand that her dreams of romance and falling in love were not his. She would get it that his plans for himself lay in a different direction. It would be a salutary learning curve that would succeed where explanations had in the past failed.

'My mother is a firm believer in true love and happy-ever-after endings,' Lucas intoned with a corrosive cynicism he made no attempt to disguise. 'She married the man she fell in love with as a teenager and they stayed married and in love until the day he died. She has high hopes that I might continue the tradition and she doesn't see it happening in the arms of any of the supermodels I've ever dated.'

'There's nothing wrong with true love and happy-ever-after endings. You might have had *one* bad experience, but you can't knock the real thing because of that.'

'I'm surprised to hear you say that after what you've been through.' But he wasn't. She struck him as just the sort of hopeless romantic who nurtured secret dreams of the walk down the aisle in a big wedding dress, with a sprawling line of best-friend bridesmaids in her wake. The sort of girl who eagerly looked forward to testing her culinary skills in her very own kitchen while lots of little Millies pitter-pattered at her feet. Just the sort of girl his mother imagined for him and precisely the sort of girl he would run a mile from, because he'd had his learning curve when it came to all that nonsense about love.

'Just because I was let down—'

'Dumped by a guy who absconded with your best friend.'

Milly flushed hotly. 'There's no need to ram that down my throat.'

'A little reality goes a long way, Milly.'

'If by that you mean that it goes a long way to turning me into someone who doesn't believe in love and marriage, then I'd rather not face it.'

'Well, considering I have no time for any of that, it should be a cinch demonstrating to my mother just how incompatible we are.'

'If we're that incompatible, then I'm wondering how we ever got involved with one another in the first place,' Milly said tartly. 'I'm broken-hearted and vulnerable after a broken engagement, and you swoop into my life and decide that I'm the one for you even though I'm the last person on the planet you would get involved with? How does that make sense, Lucas?'

'Like I said, my mother is a devotee of fairy stories like that.'

'Then she doesn't know you at all, does she?'

'Do you ever accept anything without questioning it out of existence?' He shook his head and sighed with a mixture of resignation and exasperation. 'People believe what they want to believe even if evidence to the contrary is staring them in the face. My mother believes in true love without any encouragement from me, I assure you. So she won't find it odd at all that you've swept me off my feet.'

Milly blushed and looked away. 'Does she know about your experience with that girl when you were still a kid? An excusable mistake when you were too young to know better.'

'Is that your way of introducing your analysis of the experience?' He shot her a glance of brooding impatience, which she returned with unblinking disingenuousness. 'Which I'm seriously regretting telling you abou. To answer your question, no, she doesn't.' His gaze became thoughtful. 'Which brings me to one or two ground rules that should be put in place.'

'Yes?' What would it take to sweep a man like Lucas off his feet? she wondered. Someone amazing. And that person existed, even if he didn't think so. His parents had been happily married, as had hers. Her grandmother had told her numerous tales of how much in love her parents had been. Inseparable, she had said. Growing up, Milly had never tired of looking at snapshots of them together; had never tired of hearing all the small details of the childhood sweethearts who had grown up together and had never wavered in their love for one another. Maybe those tales had formed the person she was now: idealistic and eternally hopeful that she would one day find the right guy for her.

If it was inconceivable that someone like Lucas, jaded and cynical, could ever be attracted to someone like her, then it was equally inconceivable that someone like her, optimistic and romantic, could ever be attracted to someone like him.

'Ground rules...' he repeated gently, snapping her out of her reverie.

'Oh, yes, you were about to tell me.'

'Ground rule number one,' he said, frowning, because never had he ever had to work so hard at getting a woman's attention, 'is the importance of remembering that this is just a temporary charade.'

Milly looked at him, eyes wide with puzzlement. 'I know *that*.'

'By which,' Lucas continued, taking advantage of her full, concentrated attention before she could drift off into one of those doubtless cotton-candy fantasies of hers, 'I mean that you don't get ideas.'

'What on earth are you talking about?' Enlightenment dawned as he stared at her with unflinching intent. 'Oh, I get it,' she said slowly, as colour crept into her face and her heart picked up angry speed. 'You don't want me to start thinking that the game is for real. You really are the limit! Do you honestly imagine for a second that I would be stupid enough to fall for a guy like you? Especially after everything you've told me?'

'Come again?'

'You think that because you happen to be okay looking, because you happen to have a lot of money, somehow you're an irresistible catch! And you may just be for all those supermodel women who like being draped over your arm, getting their pictures taken whenever they're with you, but I meant it when I told you that I can't think of anything worse! Least of all with a guy who's said that he sees marriage as a business transaction!'

'Sure about that?' Lucas's mouth thinned, a reaction to the unfamiliar sound of criticism.

'Quite sure,' Milly informed him scathingly. 'I could never be interested in a man like you. I'm sure you have wonderful qualities…' She paused for a heartbeat while she tried to imagine what those wonderful qualities might be. Certainly sensitivity and thoughtfulness didn't feature too high.

Although, a little voice pointed out, *isn't his attitude towards his mother an indication of just those qualities, lurking there somewhere underneath the cool, hard, jaded exterior?*

'But,' she continued hurriedly, 'I go for caring, sharing fun guys.'

'Caring? Sharing? Fun? This may come as a shock, but when it comes to fun I can't think of a single woman who's ever complained.'

'I'm not talking about *sex,*' Milly said derisively, scarlet-faced, because really what on earth did she know about sex? Her life had not exactly been littered with panting suitors desperate to strip her naked and climb into bed with her. Sure, there had been interest. She had even gone out with a couple of them. But none of those brief relationships had ever stayed the course. Either she was too fussy or she just wasn't clever enough to play the games that most women knew how to play, the games that trapped men. Not that she had ever had any inclination to trap any of the guys she had dated briefly.

She went a shade pinker as she wondered how Lucas

would react if he knew that she was a virgin. The virgin and the rake, poles apart, the most unlikely pretend couple in the world!

'I'm talking about the sort of caring, giving man who shares the same belief system as I do; the sort of man who wants the same things that I want—love, friendship, a soulmate for life…'

'Sounds thrilling,' Lucas said drily. 'You're omitting passion. Or is that sidelined by the friendship, soulmate angle?' He shot her a wolfish grin that made her skin prickle, made it difficult to keep her eyes focused on his lean, dark face. 'Never mind, I get the picture, and I'm glad that we're singing from the same song sheet. That being the case, you will have no need to pretend. I imagine our conflicting personalities will be enough to demonstrate to my mother that our relationship is not destined to last longer than it takes for you to rustle up a hot meal.' He shrugged elegantly and shot her a crooked smile. 'Feel free to share all your home truths about me!'

'I most certainly will! And…one other thing.' The plane began dipping, preparing to land. 'I'm afraid I didn't come prepared for warm weather.' She thought wistfully of the innocent little ski-resort job she had mapped out as part of her recovery programme. 'I hadn't expected to find myself on a plane to Madrid.'

'Believe it or not, there are shops there. A free wardrobe is part of the package.'

'I don't feel comfortable with that.'

'Then we can agree on a repayment schedule—although you might want to settle into your new job when you get back to London before you start working out how to transfer money into my account for a handful of clothes.'

'I wonder how it is that I never spotted just how *infuriating* you could be.'

'That could certainly be one of the things you tell my mother that you dislike about me,' Lucas pointed out. 'Although who knows how she might react to the shock of hearing a woman speak her mind? You have to bear in mind that she's had a stroke.'

'You're telling me that no one ever speaks their mind when they're around you?'

'Frankly, no. Although you're more than making up for that.'

The small plane touched down smoothly, skimming over the landing strip like a little wasp before slowly grinding to a halt. Conversation was abandoned amidst the business of disembarking, after which a long, sleek car was waiting for them, complete with uniformed driver.

Cool, early spring temperatures greeted them. She was fine in what she was wearing but, stepping into the car, which was the height of luxury, she was suddenly and acutely aware of just not quite blending into her surroundings. What was appropriate gear for travelling in a luxury chauffeur-driven limo? She was sure that there would be some sort of dress code and, whatever it was, it certainly wasn't what she was wearing. His mother might disapprove of supermodel girlfriends, but supermodel girlfriends would match expensive limos; supermodel girlfriends would pull off luxury houses and private planes...

And suddenly she felt that tug of self-consciousness that had been her occasional companion growing up—the little pang of knowing that she really wasn't too sure when it came to the opposite sex, of knowing that she would never really make it into the inner sanctum of the cool set, even though she got along just fine with them. Lucas's mother might have whimsical dreams about her son finding a suitably wholesome, down-to-earth girl but she would discover fast enough that wholesome, down-to-earth girls were not fashioned for ridiculously wealthy lifestyles.

Her eyes slid across to where he was sitting, casually at ease in his expensive limo. His sense of style was so much a part of him that he could have been wearing a bin bag and he would still have looked stupendously sophisticated. Stupendously sophisticated and utterly, bone-meltingly, sinfully *sexy*.

He was right. There would be no need for her to pretend because there was no way his mother could fail to notice just how ill-suited they were as a couple. She wouldn't be deceiving anyone. She would just have to be herself. This was going to be a little adventure, nothing to get all worked up and anxious about. Life threw curve balls and she was catching one. When again would she find herself in this position—freed from all responsibility; no job, nothing waiting for her back in London, suddenly free to do exactly what she wanted to do?

She rested her head back and half-closed her eyes, and when she turned to look at him after a few seconds it was to find him staring right back at her. He had the darkest eyes imaginable and lashes most women would kill for. The perfect, beautiful symmetry of his lean face should have made him too…*pretty,* but there was a harsh, dangerous strength there that made him 100 percent alpha male.

Her heart skipped a beat. She was supposed to be romantically involved with the guy! What a joke. As though someone like him would ever look at someone like her! Even that gold-digger who hadn't been a supermodel had probably *looked* like one. But for a few heart-stopping seconds she imagined what it might feel like to be touched by him; to be seduced by that rich, dark, dangerous, velvety voice; to have him run his hands over her naked body.

She bit back a stifled gasp as moisture pooled between her legs and a heavy, tingling ache began in her breasts and coursed through her body until she felt hot and uncomfortable in her skin.

It was a physical reaction that was so unexpected and so blindingly powerful that she felt faint. Faint, giddy and slightly sick. She couldn't remember feeling anything like this when she had been with Robbie. In fact, she couldn't remember feeling anything like this *ever.* She was shockingly aware of her own body in a way she never had been before, aware that she wanted it to be *touched,* wanted the strange tickle between her legs to be alleviated.

She dragged her eyes away from his mesmerising face, mortified at the suspicion that he could see exactly what was going through her head, and even more mortified when she belatedly remembered what he had said about making sure she didn't start getting ideas.

'How long before we get, er, to your mother's house?' she asked because talking might distract her from what was going on with her body.

A little over an hour. An hour of sitting next to him in the limo, trying hard to rein in her wandering mind. An hour of pretending not to notice the muscled strength of his forearms; the taut pull of his trousers over his powerful thighs; the length of his fingers; the sexiness of his mouth; the way his voice curled around her, tantalising, tempting, as velvety smooth as the finest dark chocolate.

Every confusing sensation racing through her body

and running like quicksilver through her head crystal-
lised to demonstrate, conclusively, just how inexperienced she was when it came to the opposite sex. And,
as if that wasn't bad enough, she couldn't even rely on
good old common sense to point her in the right direction or else she wouldn't be sitting here, pressed against
the car door to create maximum space between them,
babbling like the village idiot because it was better than
letting any disturbing silences settle between them.

At the end of half an hour she knew more about Madrid than she did about her own village where she had
grown up because she had plied him with questions. By
the time they were drawing into Salamanca, she could
have done a doctorate on the subject.

Not only did his mother have a house in Salamanca
but she also had a house in Madrid for those times
when she fancied an extended shopping trip to the city,
or when she visited friends and wanted somewhere to
stay over.

It hadn't been used in a while because ill health had
interrupted her usual routine, she had been told.

'Relax,' Lucas told her wryly. She was staring at
him, mouth parted on the brink of yet another question. There seemed to be no end to them. He politely
refrained from telling her that he had never known any
woman to talk as much as she did. 'You're not walking
into a dragon's den.'

'I didn't think I was,' Milly lied.

'Oh, yes, you did. That's why you haven't drawn
breath since you started asking me to give you a ver-
bal guided tour of Madrid and its surroundings. If we'd
been in the car for another hour, you would probably
have extended your parameters to the rest of Spain, because you think that talking calms your nerves.'

'I'm not nervous. We've agreed that neither of us has to pretend to be anything other than what we are.'

'You're nervous. And you're the girl who wasn't nervous when she was plying me with questions about my past. Don't be.' He gently tilted her chin away from him, directing her to look through the front window, and her eyes widened at the mansion approaching them. She had barely noticed when the limo had pulled off the main road. 'We're here.'

Milly's mouth dropped open. The low white house with its red roof sprawled gloriously amidst a profusion of shrubs, flowers and trees. The intense blue of the sky picked up the even more intense, vibrant colours of the clambering flowers of every shape and variety, and everything melded harmoniously together into picture-postcard perfection.

Standing at the front door was a tall, striking woman leaning on a walking stick. Black hair was pulled back from an angular, handsome face.

'I have no idea why my mother can't let one of the maids get the door.' But there was affectionate indulgence in his voice and Milly had a vivid image of the boy beneath the man, the unguarded person beneath the cynical, hard-edged adult in control of an empire. He was a loving son and she had a moment of piercing happiness that she had agreed to this unexpected charade.

'She probably just can't wait to see you.'

'To see *us*...' The limo swerved smoothly to a halt and, as they emerged from the car, she felt the heavy weight of his arm sling over her shoulders. 'We are, after all, the loving couple,' he whispered into her ear and the warmth of his breath made her want to squirm. 'At least before the rot sets in...' And, to prove his point, he curved his hand under her hair to caress the nape of her neck.

And then, barely breaking stride, with such natural-ness that anyone would have been forgiven for thinking that what they had was real, he paused, dipped his head and covered her mouth lightly with his.

Just a brief meeting of tongues, enough to do dev-astating things to her body, then he was pulling away, hand still caressing her neck. The epitome of a man in love.

He couldn't have been more successful at killing her nerves because how could she be nervous about facing his mother when her thoughts were all over the place at that what that casual kiss had done to her body…?

CHAPTER SEVEN

ANTONIA ROMERO WAS an elegant, quietly spoken woman who immediately put Milly at ease. She ushered them in warmly, allowing Lucas to kiss her on the cheek and then fret at the fact that she had come to the door herself when she should be resting, when there was help in the house to do things like answer doors.

'I just couldn't wait to meet Milly…' she protested, drawing Milly into the living room, where tea and pastries were waiting for them on a low glass table while a pretty, smiling maid hovered in the background, ready to leap to service. 'And I know you must be tired after your trip but I'm dying to hear all about your romance. I knew it. I just knew that son of mine would end up finding true love with a real woman and not one of those plastic dolls he's spent his life fooling around with.'

Milly sneaked a surreptitious look at Lucas to see how he was handling his mother's criticism and he caught her eye and grinned, eyebrows raised.

'Didn't I tell you that my mother has no problem saying exactly what she thinks?' He shooed Antonia back to the sofa as she automatically rose to pour them tea and hand round the pastries. On cue, the maid leaped into action and refreshments were served before the maid vanished out of the room, shutting the door behind her.

With Antonia on the low, damask pink sofa facing her, Milly had a chance really to look at her hostess. There were fine lines of strain around her eyes and mouth and she was borderline too thin, barely filling the black, shapeless dress that hung down to her calves, yet it wasn't hard to see that she must have been a great beauty in her day. Not that she was exactly ancient now. At a guess, Milly would have put her in her mid to late sixties.

She tried to maintain the chirpy smile of a woman in love as Lucas helped himself to a few more pastries before subsiding right next to her on the sofa, a replica of the one on which Antonia was sitting, his thigh pressed against hers.

She had been leaning forward, perched on the edge of the sofa, her hand primly linked on her knees, and now he pulled her back so that she tumbled against him.

'What would you like to know?' Lucas's voice was teasing as he fondly addressed his mother. 'You have limited time for questions because you should be taking it easy.'

'I'm sitting,' Antonia retorted, smiling. 'How much easier can I take things? Please don't join the queue along with all my friends who have insisted on treating me with kid gloves ever since I got ill.'

'Why don't you explain…?' Lucas brushed aside Milly's hair and delivered a feathery kiss on the side of her cheek, just enough to send the heat spiralling through her.

Milly's eyes glazed over. If she wasn't under a microscope, she would have punched him, because he was the one who had propelled her into this awkward situation; how fair was it that she was now being dumped in the thick of it, having to concoct some vaguely realistic lie? Not very.

Antonia was watching her expectantly and Milly reluctantly stumbled into a suitable tale of sudden love and searing romance. She swept aside the minor detail of her broken engagement as just a bit of nonsense from which she had thankfully escaped because, had she not, how else would she have found herself with Lucas? Fate.

Good word. Antonia picked up the cue and reminisced over her own wonderful marriage. Fate had thrown her and her husband together from such a young age.

How could Milly resist confiding about her own parents, also childhood sweethearts? She couldn't. They had died too young but desperately in love; she felt scared at the thought of being deserted by those she loved, but she still believed in love with all her heart, whatever the risks it brought. She was thinking of Lucas and the mystery gold-digger when she said that. Belatedly, as Antonia nodded approvingly, Milly remembered that this was not supposed to be a bonding experience. She cleared her throat and wondered whether she should shove the man at her side into picking up the baton and continuing their fictional tale of love.

'Of course.' She decided against that course of action because who knew what he would say? He hadn't uttered a peep while she had been in confiding mode, although she had felt him edge a little closer to her, all the better to...*what*? Prolong his mother's incorrect assumptions? 'Wonderful though our sudden love is, I have to admit that your son can be a little...*forceful*.'

'Too forceful?' Antonia asked, and Milly ruefully inclined her head to one side, as though seriously giving the question house room, before erring on the side of tactful.

'Borderline arrogant,' she sighed, patting Lucas's thigh without looking at him. 'I guess it's something to do with having grown up in the lap of luxury. I'm afraid I grew up in the lap of, well, rubbing pennies together and trying to make ends meet…' She left Antonia to make the obvious deduction, which was that they were worlds apart and therefore incompatible in a fundamental area. The first of many, if only she knew.

Antonia seemed delighted with her admission. 'So good,' she murmured, tearing up, 'that you've finally come to your senses…' she smiled at her son and leaned forward '…and realised how much more fulfilling it is to have a real woman at your side. My dear, let me tell you about my dearest husband and myself. We rubbed many a penny together before Roberto's career began to take off! I could tell you a hundred tales of having to choose between paying the bills and buying food, especially in the beginning when we owed the bank so much money…'

'Thank you so much for helping me out there,' was the first thing Milly said when, an hour and three pastries later, they were being ushered up to their bedrooms. 'Why didn't you…why didn't you…?'

'Launch into a speech about why our fast and furious romance is destined to crash and burn within the next fortnight?'

He hadn't known about how she felt about her background. Orphaned as a kid and brought up by her grandmother, yet never looking back and blaming an unfortunate past. Still believing in the power of love even though abandonment issues should have made her wary and cynical, disinclined ever to trust anyone to get too close. Still ever-hopeful, the eternal optimist.

He had known women who had been blessed with the best life could offer and still managed to moan and complain about nothing in particular.

'Bit soon for the cracks to be showing, wouldn't you agree?'

At the top of the landing, the maid turned right and they both followed, Lucas breaking off to say something to the maid in rapid-fire Spanish that had her laughing. Their cases had been brought up whilst they had been in the sitting room.

'Your mother's really lovely,' Milly admitted. 'It's going to be a shame when she has to face up to the fact that you're so obnoxious that no one in their right mind would ever put up with you.'

Lucas looked down to see whether she was joking, but her expression was thoughtful and earnest.

'There are times when I can't actually believe that I'm hearing what you say correctly.'

Milly stopped and looked at him with a little frown. 'Do you have any idea how arrogant you were when you led me to believe that you were someone you weren't? I may only have been the chalet girl, but you just didn't see why you should be honest with me. For a start, you assumed that I was the sort of low life who would be out to see what I could get if I knew you were rich, and then you just didn't give a damn if you weren't honest. You didn't care about my feelings at all. I know you had one bad experience with a gold-digger but that's no excuse to just assume that everyone falls into the same category, guilty until proved innocent.'

'How did your feelings have anything to do with... anything at all?'

'You barely apologised for having duped me,' Milly told him flatly.

Where had that come from? Lucas, frustrated, raked his fingers through his hair and stared at her, lost for words.

'You just *assumed* that it was okay because you can do what you want to do without bothering to consider other people.'

'Is this conversation going anywhere?' he questioned in a driven voice. He glared at the maid, who seemed to be suppressing a smirk.

'I'm projecting…'

'You're *what*? I have no idea what you're talking about.'

'I'm projecting ahead to when you mother sadly discovers what a selfish, self-centred guy you've turned out to be.'

'I'm guessing she's probably wised up to those traits a while ago,' Lucas said drily, eyebrows raised. 'And, while we're on the subject of scrupulous honesty and caring about the feelings of others, have you mentioned to your grandmother what's going on in this part of the world?'

Milly flushed. 'I didn't see any point in worrying her by going into details.' It wasn't as though this was going to be a long-term situation. Two weeks—three, absolute max—he had told her when she had agreed to his plan. In those weeks, even if a dramatic break-up hadn't been staged, they should have covered the important phase of their fairy-tale romance revealing shaky foundations.

In those couple of weeks, he had privately thought, his mother would put to bed all ideas of trying to see him settled with the woman of her dreams. She would kill off notions of fairy-tale romances insofar as they pertained to him and she would resign herself to cheerful acceptance that what he wanted out of life, emotionally, was a far cry from what she thought would do him good.

She was his mother and he indulged her but, at the end of it, it was his life and he would choose its outcome whether or not it flew in the face of her ideals. This exercise in harmless fiction would be a gentle learning curve for her.

'I'm only going to be here for a short while and, when I return to London and my life's all sorted out, maybe then I'll let her in on some of the details.'

'You honestly think your life's going to be *all sorted out* when you return to London?'

'You said that…'

Lucas waved aside her predictable cry of protest. He had offered to have a formal agreement drawn up listing the conditions of this arrangement, what she would be given at the end of it, but she had airily told him that that wouldn't be necessary.

'I'm not talking about the job and the accommodation and the money, Milly. I'm talking about your blind faith in life always turning out for the best.'

'I don't have to listen to this.' She turned away and felt his hand gently stay her.

'If my mother's long overdue a little learning curve, then you should take this opportunity to put in place one of your own. Reality doesn't disappear because you decide that you'd quite like it to.' He nodded to the maid, who had tactfully moved to stare through one of the sprawling windows on the landing, ears blocked to any conversation—although Milly didn't think she spoke a word of English, so that probably was a step too far when it came to fulfilling her unspoken duties.

Milly watched, mouth open in anger, as he sauntered off, once again speaking Spanish, once again making the maid giggle. The maid might have been an old retainer well into her sixties, but it was obvious that he could still work the charm offensive on her.

Which was something he couldn't be bothered doing in *her* case.

How dared he think that he could bring his jaundiced views to bear on *her* life?

Placid by nature, she could scarcely credit the fury bubbling up inside her as her brain began functioning once again, and she tripped along behind him, barely paying attention to the magnificent surroundings.

The house was in the style of a rambling ranch. A short flight of stairs led up to the first floor, which, like the floor below, was wooden-floored, the wood gleaming from years of polish.

The corridor opened out in places into small sitting areas and curved round in other places, leading to nooks and crannies, various bedrooms and sitting rooms. It should have been disjointed and higgledy-piggledy but in fact there was an attractive coherence about the honeycomb nature of the layout, something whimsical and charming.

A lot of light poured in, thanks to large windows at regular intervals, a couple of which were fashioned of stained glass so that the bright sunlight was refracted into thousands of splintered shapes.

Through the windows, as she marched along in Lucas's wake, she could see extensive lawns and the bright turquoise of a swimming pool.

She stopped behind Lucas as the maid disappeared

into one of the bedrooms and she hovered, arms folded, still simmering.

'Good news and bad news.'

'Huh?' Snapping out of her reverie, Milly focused on his swarthy, handsome face. He leaned against the doorframe, the very picture of cool elegance.

'The good news is that it's a vast bedroom, complete with two sofas. There are even twin wardrobes. The bad news is that we're sharing it.'

The maid had vanished and Milly stared at Lucas, heat flooding her cheeks.

'You told me that there was no way your mother was going to…going to stick us in the room together! You told me that your mother was very old-fashioned, that she hadn't been brought up on a diet of sex before marriage. You *said* that she might know what you got up to but she'd always been adamant that you wouldn't get up to it under *her roof.*'

'I have a feeling that on those occasions when I showed up with a woman in tow she decided that the best way to avoid contributing to a loveless union was to locate us at opposite ends of the house.'

'Is that all you can say?' Milly hissed as her anger headed a little bit further north.

'At the moment, yes.' He pushed himself away from the doorframe and strolled into the guest suite.

Normally, he was given his usual room in the other wing of the house. He had barely noticed that they were being shown to a room in the opposite direction.

'How is this supposed to work?' Milly persisted, hands on hips as she followed him through.

'You should shut the door. The last thing we need is for wagging ears to hear us at each other's throats.'

'I thought that that was supposed to be the whole intention.'

'Not on day one. Now shut the door, Milly.'

'Bossy,' she muttered, stepping into the room with the unwillingness of someone entering a torture chamber.

How was she supposed to share a room with the man standing in front of her? How could he look so cool and collected when she was suddenly a bundle of nervous tension?

'You might want to freshen up,' Lucas said neutrally. He nodded in the direction of the *en suite* bathroom, which she saw was as big as the bedroom, which was huge.

'We can't share a room.'

'I won't be breaking that to my mother at this point in time, Milly, so you might as well settle into the idea. What's the problem anyway?'

'The problem is that I don't even *know* you...'

'It wasn't a problem when we were in Courchevel,' Lucas pointed out with infuriating logic. 'And frankly, thanks to your reckless habit of saying what you want and asking whatever questions you choose to ask, you probably know me a lot better than most.' And that was a shocking revelation. But true. A certain, intangible unease snaked through him.

'We weren't sharing a *bedroom* there. We were sharing a *mansion*.'

'But, on the upside, at least now you know that I'm not a homicidal maniac or a ski instructor on the lookout for a body to take to bed.'

'I didn't sign up for this.'

'For what, exactly?' His voice was silky smooth and those midnight-dark eyes watching her speculatively made her feel hot and tingly all over.

All those forbidden thoughts that had crowded into her head from the very first moment she had laid eyes on him surfaced with frightening ease.

Thoughts of him touching her, tasting her; crazy, stupid thoughts that were just the product of a fevered mind unbalanced by the trauma of a broken engagement.

Except, when was the last time she had thought about Robbie? How traumatised had she really been, exactly? If her heart had been broken, wouldn't she have still been cooped up somewhere, licking her wounds and thinking about a future that wasn't going to happen?

'Cling to the prospect of what you're getting out of this,' he advised her. 'And, if it puts your mind at ease, I'm happy to take the couch.' He'd contemplated the enticing prospect of taking her to bed—before she had discovered who he really was and all the advantages that came wrapped up with him. She might make a big deal of her maidenly virtue, but how long would it be before she began really looking round his mother's mansion; before she heard about all the other houses he owned, scattered across the globe like unused jewels waiting to be aired when the occasion arose?

Take one self-confessed romantic, tie it up with a broken heart and then into the mix throw one billionaire with a healthy libido and what did you come out with?

Complications. It didn't take a genius to figure that one out. And, when it came to complications of an emotional nature, well, that was something Lucas could do without.

So if that quirky *something* about her got to him…if there was something about her unruly hair and sexy little body that got his imagination firing on all cylinders…he would have to put it to rest. He was accustomed to getting exactly what he wanted with the opposite sex but, in this instance, his hands were tied and he wasn't about to untie them so that he could play with a bit of fire.

Milly eyed the couch with jaundiced eyes. Okay, so he wouldn't be sharing the bed with her—the gigantic king-size bed with its gauze canopy—but she would still be *aware* of him sleeping only a matter of metres away.

And that shouldn't be a problem. *He* certainly didn't see it as one. Maybe he had flirted slightly with her, in his few days as a ski instructor, but that was then.

'I'm not accustomed to sharing a bedroom,' she protested feebly and his face relaxed into a disbelieving, mocking half smile.

'You were engaged…' He drew that one sentence out as though it was explanation in itself that she wasn't quite telling the truth.

Milly reddened, mouth dry. 'You keep reminding me of that,' she said in a valiant attempt to change the course of the conversation because she didn't like where it was heading. 'I guess in a minute you'll start lecturing me about not facing reality and being a hopeless romantic and burying my head in the sand…'

Lucas narrowed his eyes on her. 'You didn't share a bedroom with the guy?' he asked, honing in on the truth with deadly accuracy. He watched the way she guiltily glazed over and licked her lips. He knew that he shouldn't pursue the topic because, frankly, there was no point. This wasn't a 'getting to know you' exercise, after all, although stable doors and horses sprang to mind, resuscitating that unease he had earlier felt. *They knew each other… Like it or not, weird though it seemed…*

'I don't think that's any of your business,' Milly said

haughtily. 'And I think I'll have that shower you mentioned...'

'Course it's my business,' he told her with just the sort of slow smile that implied that shrewd mind of his was leaping to all sorts of correct conclusions about her relationship with Robbie. 'We're in love. Isn't that what star-struck lovers do— share everything?'

'You...you're...' She spluttered furiously at him and he grinned.

'You're like a little spitting cat.'

'If your mother was a fly on the wall, she'd get a pretty good picture of how *not* star-struck lovers are!' She could all but get the words out. The man was infuriating! There wasn't a human being on the planet who could work her up so fast and so effortlessly.

'Or...' Lucas held her gaze but he was still grinning '...she might decide that a little volatility is good when it comes to...being in love and star- struck...'

'Well, she'd be wrong,' Milly hissed, making a bee-line for her case and rummaging until she had located some clothes. 'And now, if you don't mind, I'm going to have a bath.'

Sure you don't want me to join you? The instinctive riposte was on the tip of his tongue but then the thought of actually doing that, of actually sliding into the warm water with her, soaping her, feeling her curves pressed against him, slammed into him with the force of a runaway train and his mouth tightened.

'I have work to do,' he said abruptly. 'Take your time. Dinner's usually served around seven-thirty. Early by Spanish standards but my mother's schedule is no longer what it was. I'll either come and get you, take you down to the dining room, or I'll dispatch one of the maids to show you the way.'

Running a bath, door firmly locked, Milly figured that this was how it must feel like to be a toy at the whim of an unpredictable owner. He had managed to rile her, provoke her and then, when it felt as though she actually *needed* to have some sort of full-blown argument with him, needed to wipe that annoying, laid-back grin from his face, he changed, just like that, for no particular reason.

Boredom.

She eased herself into the bath and closed her eyes. He had suddenly become bored. He enjoyed provoking her and he knew he could. It amused him. But, like a kid with the attention span of a flea, his amusement had a very short sell-by date because, however *different* he might find her, she just didn't have what it took to hold his attention for longer than five seconds. Thank goodness this was all just a fabrication! Because if it wasn't then she would never be good enough for him, would she? Being *different* didn't count. Being a *novelty* didn't count.

She mentioned that over dinner. A fabulous dinner served by a different maid. A typically Spanish meal of paella rich with seafood with lots of salad. Just a casual little remark when there was a lull in the conversation, a little throwaway observation about her *sheer amazement* that she and Lucas had become involved, because they were just so different, because she was just the sort of girl he would find boring…

Antonia had smiled and talked about opposites attracting and then, sensing something intense in Milly's expression, had kindly listed all the ways that relationships worked when two people complemented each other by bringing different personality traits to the union.

Lucas had failed to take the bait with the opening. Was he still of the opinion that his mother should have a honeymoon period before the cracks began showing?

When Milly thought of that bedroom, waiting for them to share it, she was of the opinion that the cracks should surface sooner rather than later.

She thought so even more when, over coffee in the sitting room, yet another room new to her, he draped his arm over her shoulders, sitting next to her with the indolent casualness of a man with his woman. His low, sexy voice was warm and teasing. He absently played with her hair. When she spoke, she could feel his breath warm on her cheek as he looked at her.

Antonia was taking in everything, eyes shrewd, and if *he* didn't see that then Milly certainly did and it was the very first thing she said to him when Antonia excused herself for the night, leaving the two of them alone in the sitting room.

'You *could* have helped me out when I began listing all the reasons why we didn't make sense as a couple.' She sprang to her feet and plonked herself down on a chair far away from him although, even though there was now distance between them, she could still feel the weight of his arm around her and the warmth of his thigh pressed against hers.

'Did you *see* your mother? She thought it was *cute* that I was pointing out all our differences!'

Lucas shrugged and Milly gritted her pearly-white teeth in pure frustration.

He hadn't seen his mother this happy in a while. How long had she been secretly harbouring hopes that he would meet the woman of his dreams and bring her home? She had dropped hints in the past but she had really only begun pressing him after her illness. But had she been fretting long before then?

'The time isn't right for a two-pronged attack.'

'There's no question of an *attack*.' Why did he have to be so dramatic? she wondered. Why did he have to make her out as the bad guy in this when she was only here because of him and only gently laying the foundations for their break-up because that was what she had been primed to do?

'And,' she continued, 'I'd rather you didn't sit so close to me...'

'Sit so *close* to you?'

'I just think that your mother might find such public displays of affection a little embarrassing, that's all.'

'We're sharing a bedroom. Somehow I don't think she's going to swoon because I stroke your thigh now and again. Did she look embarrassed?'

'That's not the point.'

'The point is, I have no idea what you're talking about. I'm not going to retreat to the furthest corner of the room. That would be unnatural. Furthermore, I don't see why it's such a big deal.'

'The big deal,' Milly said with a ferocious whisper, because how could he be so *cool* when she was all over the place? 'Is that I'm still in the process of getting over something pretty big and pretty horrible and maybe I need just a little more physical space than you're giving me. Lord knows what your mother must secretly think of me.' A sudden thought occurred to her. 'What if she thinks I'm a gold-digger? After all, one minute I'm engaged to one guy and the next minute I'm going out with a billionaire.' She wrung her hands in despair at the misconception.

'What if she thinks I *targeted* you...? It makes horrible sense in a way, doesn't it? What if she imagines that I'm just one of a long line of women who want you for what you can do for them...?'

Lucas raised his eyebrows and held up one imperious hand to stop her before she could begin exploring this new theme in exhaustive depth.

'She doesn't think that,' he told her flatly. 'Nor does she think that you're somehow emotionally unstable and fickle because you're going out with me hard on the heels of a broken engagement.'

'You can't say that.'

'Oh, but I can and I have.'

'What do you mean *you have*?'

'I told my mother that this was not a case of you jumping from one man to another without pausing for breath. I've explained that I'm not a rebound love affair—which, as you can imagine, would not have sat well with her.'

'When did all this explaining take place?' Milly asked in frank bemusement.

'When you were soaking in the bath for two hours,' Lucas said drily. *She thinks you're impossibly brave. As I do...*

'And she believed you?' Milly aimed for an incredulous laugh. 'I know you could sell ice to Eskimos, Lucas, but women are very intuitive when it comes to stuff like that; when it comes to matters of *the heart*...'

'Which is why she knows it's the truth,' Lucas told her with silky assurance. 'She's met you, talked to you and she knows—like we both do, Milly—that whatever you had with your ex-fiancé wasn't love. You may be the jilted girlfriend, and that's not a great place to be, but you're not the heartbroken jilted girlfriend. So your little speech about feeling uncomfortable sitting too close to me because you're nursing a broken heart is, frankly, a load of rubbish. Maybe you're scared of being too close to me because you think I'm going to make a move on you...'

And hadn't the thought crossed his head more than once? *Good job he had iron self-discipline and was smart enough to spot danger before it spotted him.*

'Not going to happen. Or maybe,' he mused thoughtfully, 'you're scared because you think *you* might make a move on *me...*'

Milly could feel herself burning up as he shoved his version of reality down her throat. There was nothing he said that had not occurred to her before, even if only in passing.

And that included the shameful fact that she found the man physically attractive, that she had flirted with silly fantasies...

'In your dreams,' she told him tartly. But she heard the faint wobble in her voice. She wasn't accustomed to playing these sorts of games. She was straightforward; she had never found herself in this kind of situation. She was walking in unchartered territory and it was only her survivor's instinct that told her that, whatever she did, she should not show him that he was right. That maybe, just maybe, that bed held unspoken terrors for her because she could picture, far too easily, what it might be like *to have him in it next to her...*

CHAPTER EIGHT

MILLY GAZED AT her reflection in the mirror but she wasn't really focusing on the face staring back at her. She was thinking of the past week and a half.

Behind her, the king-size bed that had filled her with horror was just…a king-sized bed. Her fears had been unjustified. At least, unjustified except in the deepest, darkest corners of her mind where fantasies of Lucas still swirled around with dangerous strength, powerful riptides lying in wait for the appropriate moment to suck her under, or so it felt.

They barely shared this private space. Antonia always retired before ten, at which point Milly would head upstairs, leaving Lucas downstairs, where he would work until the early hours of the morning. She neither heard nor saw him when he finally made it to the bedroom because she was always sound asleep. The only evidence he left that he occupied the room at all was the barely discernible imprint on the sofa where he had slept, because he was always up and moving by eight in the morning.

The man hardly needed any sleep at all. She, on the other hand, had always been able to sleep for England.

The linen he used for the sofa was always shoved neatly in the wardrobe.

Twice she had woken needing the bathroom and her heart had been pounding as she had tiptoed her way past where he had lain sprawled and asleep, half-naked, the thin duvet barely covering him.

That fleeting glimpse of him sadly had been yet more fodder for her very active imagination.

If only this stupid charade had done what it should have done and exposed his failings. At this point in time, shouldn't he have morphed into an arrogant bore with too much money for his own good? Shouldn't the impact of his good looks have done her a favour by diminishing?

She sighed and peered a little more closely at her reflection. The hair looked wilder than usual but she had given up trying to tame it. Was this the look she really wanted to go for? Wild hair and a strappy dress, and high-heeled sandals that were *so* not her thing?

She and Lucas, at his mother's urging, were going to have a supposedly romantic dinner out tonight. She had given Milly a stern talk on buying something pretty for the occasion, because she had not been shopping, and had managed to use what she had brought with her: jeans; T-shirts; more jeans; jogging bottoms.

So, despite lots of protests, she and Antonia had spent much of the day out. There had been no need to venture further afield into Madrid because Salamanca boasted designer shops for every taste. These were just the sort of things that were undermining the 'cracks in the relationship' that should have been happening by now.

Every crack Milly tried to break was papered over by Antonia, who seemed to think that her outspokenness was a charming and refreshing change from all the limpets who had cluttered her son's life before.

And in the meantime, while all this was going on, she was seeing sides to Lucas that chipped away at her defences.

He was ferociously intelligent and, whilst he was good at listening to other sides of an argument, he liked to win. Over dinner—which was usually when she saw most of him, because his days were spent working to make up for the fact that he wasn't actually in his office or on a plane going to meetings somewhere or other across the globe—they talked about everything under the sun. Antonia might generate the topic, but they would all contribute. And the topics flowed from one to another, from what was happening in the news to what had happened in the news, sometimes years previously.

He was a loving son without being patronising. He was very good at teasing his mother, and Milly's heart always constricted when she witnessed this interplay between them.

Of course, she and her grandmother were very close, as she had insisted on telling them a couple of nights ago, but it was still something to have grown up without a mother figure. Or a father figure, for that matter. She might have had a sip or two too many at this point, Milly recalled uncomfortably. She had held the floor for far too long and she might even have become a little tearful towards the end. She shuddered thinking about it.

He was also funny, witty and downright interesting. He had travelled the world. It helped when it came to recounting fascinating anecdotes about faraway places.

Her heart picked up speed as another treacherous thought crept into her head like a thief in the night: she looked forward to his company. She spent her days in the grounds, sometimes by the swimming pool reading her book, often in the company of his mother. But, when five o'clock came, she always felt a stirring in her veins, as though her body was beginning to wake up and come alive.

And that wasn't good.

In fact, it frightened her because, face it, Lucas was as distant as he had promised. Yes, when they were in each other's company he was warmth and charm itself but, the second his mother wasn't around, a shutter dropped and he became someone else. Someone cool, controlled and somehow absent.

Now, she noticed, he had stopped sitting quite so close to her on the sofa and the physical shows of affection…the little touches on her shoulder, her cheek, her arms…had dropped off.

She guessed that this was his subtle way of informing his mother that all was not quite right in the land of wonderful love and happy-ever-afters.

Had Antonia noticed? Milly didn't know. She had thought of trying to open a discussion on the subject, maybe starting with a few vague generalities before working her way up to her and Lucas and what they had, and then ending by finding out what Antonia's thoughts were. But she always chickened out because she wasn't sure she would be able to hang on to her composure if the questions became too targeted.

Right now Lucas was downstairs. He usually stopped working around six so that he could spend some time with Antonia while Milly was upstairs having a bath, changing…analysing her thoughts and coming up empty handed.

And, while Milly relaxed downstairs, usually with a glass of freshly squeezed lemonade, he took the opportunity to get cleaned up. It was a clever game of avoidance that Antonia didn't seem to notice, but Milly noticed it more and more because she was noticing *everything* more and more.

Tonight, Milly entered the sitting room to find Antonia there sipping a glass of juice, her book resting on her lap.

Like all the other rooms in the splendid house, this one was airy and light with pale walls and furnishings and adjustable wooden shutters to guard against the blistering sun during the hot summer months. And, as with all the rooms, the air was fragrant with the smell of flowers, which were cut from the garden several times a week and arranged by Antonia herself in an assortment of brightly coloured vases to be dispersed throughout the house.

'I wanted to see how the dress looked.' She beamed and beckoned Milly across and then ordered her to do a couple of turns so that she could appreciate it from every angle. 'Beautiful.'

'I don't know about that,' Milly said awkwardly. 'I'm not accustomed to wearing dresses.'

'You should. You have the perfect figure to carry them off. Not like those scrawny women my son has dated in the past. Like boys! Simpering and preening themselves and looking in every mirror they pass! *Pah!* I tell him, "Lucas, those are not real women, they are plastic dolls and you can do better than that"...' She smiled smugly and waved Milly into a chair.

'We have our differences,' Milly said weakly, determined to head off an awkward situation at the pass. 'You might think that those model types are no good for Lucas but in fact...*in fact*...they suit him far more than you might imagine. I mean...' She leaned forward and stared earnestly at the handsome woman in front of her whose head was tilted to one side, all the better to grasp what was being said because, impeccable though her English was, she still became lost in certain expressions. 'It's okay to be outspoken but, in the end, it can get on a guy's nerves.'

'Is that what happened to your last boyfriend?' Antonia asked gently. 'Was that why it all fell apart, my dear?'

Milly blushed. She had breezily and vaguely skimmed over the details of the broken engagement that had supposedly encouraged her into the arms of her one true love, Lucas. Antonia had conveniently not dwelled on the subject. Now, she was waiting for some girlish confidence.

'It fell apart,' Milly said slowly, 'Because he didn't love me and, as it turns out, I didn't love him either.' This was the first time she was actually saying aloud what she had been privately thinking. 'I was just an idiot,' she confessed. 'I'd had a crush on Robbie when I was a teenager...' She smiled, remembering the gawky, sporty kid she had been, more at home with a hockey stick than a glass of vodka, which had been the in drink at the time with all the under-age drinkers: the alcohol could be camouflaged by whatever you happened to dilute it with and parents could never tell you were actually getting a little tipsy at parties.

'Robbie was the cutest boy in the class. Floppy blond hair, gift of the gab. Plus, he would actually take time out to chat to me. It felt like love, so when he showed up in London and asked to meet up I guess I remembered what I used to feel and somehow transported it to the present day and decided that those feelings were still there, intact. He was still cute, after all. He brought back memories.'

And he had known how to manipulate her weaknesses to his own benefit but, in the end, it took two to tango. He had made inroads into her common sense because she had allowed him to.

'But what was I saying…?' She gulped back the temptation to cry just a little.

'You were saying…' Lucas's voice from behind her made her temporarily freeze '…that you got suckered in to a dud relationship with some guy who was never suited to you in the first place.'

He had been standing by the door, unnoticed by both his mother and Milly, and he couldn't quite understand just why it gave him such a kick to hear her finally admit what he had suspected all along.

She had not been occupying Heartbreak Hotel, as she had fondly and misguidedly imagined. Of course she had known that, he had seen it on her face when he had chosen to point it out to her, but it was still gratifying to hear her admit it.

Not, he hurriedly told himself, that it mattered in any way that was significant. It didn't. She might be amusing, feisty, way too open for her own good…in short, all the things he never encountered in his relationships with women…but that didn't make her available. She had been available to a simple ski instructor but to the man he was? No.

But, hell, it was getting more and more difficult by the second. He always made sure that temptation was safely out of the way by burning the midnight oil in front of his computer, although he knew that his mind was only partly on work. Too much of it, as far as he was concerned, was preoccupied with visions of her in that bed—and those visions were all the more graphic because he knew how she slept, sprawled in sexy abandon with the duvet tangled about her body.

He'd bet all his worldly possessions that that was not the way she started out. No. He imagined that she tucked herself tightly underneath those covers, *swaddled* herself in them, but somewhere along the line, when she was happily gambolling about in deep REM, her body had other ideas on how it was most comfortable. And that was not wrapped up like an Egyptian mummy.

Twice she had gone to the bathroom in the early hours of the morning, tiptoeing past the sofa in such slow motion that it had taken all he had not to burst out laughing.

Her sleepwear would be a passion-killer for most men, but the baggy T-shirt with the faded logo, reaching mid-thigh, did crazy things to his system, sent it soaring into the stratosphere. She might wear the least flattering outfits known to womankind, but her body was luscious and sexy, the jut of her full breasts promising more than a handful, the shapeliness of her legs tempting him to find out what lay between them.

He flushed darkly now as he recalled the rigid erection those thoughts had induced as he had showered.

He wondered, with some irony, whether this was what happened when the guy who could have it all was denied the one thing he found he wanted.

The sooner this charade came to an end, the better. Not least because his mother appeared to have fallen in love with the woman and that had not been on the agenda. But they were going out tonight, just the two of them, and he wouldn't mince his words.

The time for pulling the plug had come.

He was sick of waging war with his libido. He had to return to the land of the living, his offices in London. His mother was getting far too involved in their pretend love affair for his liking. And, anyway, who knew whether Milly was getting a little too accustomed to the good life? That was a consideration that had to be taken into account. Surely. Wasn't it?

'How long have you been lurking by the door?' Milly said accusingly and Lucas strolled into the room to take up position by the window, perching against the broad window sill with his arms folded.

Here comes Adonis again, Milly thought absently, *and shouldn't I have become accustomed to this by now?* She could see him a million times and still be startled by his dark, stunning beauty.

'I don't *lurk*...' His features were perfectly controlled, as was the tenor of his voice, but he had to steer firmly away from the soft swell of her breasts jutting against the soft fabric of a flimsy, strappy dress. Hell, she wasn't even wearing a bra! It bordered on indecent, even though the style was modest enough.

There was something about the shimmering colours, though...blues and creams that made the fall of her curly red hair even more vibrant...and she was wearing make-up. Just a bit. Just sufficient gloss on her full lips to tease any red-blooded man to distraction.

He felt himself harden and he looked away from her momentarily, gathering himself, before indulging in his usual light-hearted banter with his mother. The fiercer his desire grew, the more distance he had to try and put between them. Those brief touches were like matches flung onto dry tinder.

'Now, make sure you use Carlos...' his mother was telling him as he walked towards Milly, who was rising to her feet, as graceful as a ballet dancer in some strappy little sandals that showed off newly painted toenails.

'Is this the drink-driving lecture?' Lucas slipped his arm around Milly's waist and felt her soft body against his, which was a predictable challenge to his self-control. 'Don't worry. I'll be using Carlos. If I remember correctly, he has a fondness for that little wine bar not a million miles away from the restaurant. He can enjoy himself with a plate of pasta and a big bottle of mineral water.' Her breasts were just above where his hand curved on her ribcage.

As soon as they were through the front door, he dropped his hand and moved away from her.

Talk about being obvious, Milly thought, stung because he was so clearly turned off by her. She slid into the back seat through the door that Carlos held open for her and didn't glance in Lucas's direction as he levered himself in and sat next to her.

He hadn't even commented on her dress. Her normally bubbly nature was flattened by that and she was cool as they drove towards the town, choosing to stare through the window at the scenery and replying to his attempts at conversation in stiff monosyllables.

'Are you going to tell me what's wrong?' Lucas drawled once they were out of the car and in the restaurant, which was a cosy Italian that obviously appealed to the beautiful and the wealthy.

'Nothing's wrong.' Milly reluctantly looked at him and her heart picked up pace. He was staring at her, his dark eyes lazy and unfathomable. Was he comparing her to the sort of women his mother disliked but he didn't?

'Spit it out.'

'Okay—what's wrong is that you're not making any

attempt to sort this business out. We've been here nearly two weeks.'

'I didn't think you were in any rush to get back,' Lucas said mildly.

'That's not the point. The point is that I don't like lying to your mother. I feel we're getting close to one another…'

'Then make sure you pull back, Milly. She's not a substitute mother because you lost yours.'

'That's a rotten thing to say!'

Lucas sighed and raked his fingers through his hair in frustration. 'It is and for that I apologise. In actual fact, I have been thinking the same as you. It's time to start letting my mother know that this situation between us isn't going to work. For one thing, I'm sick to death of sleeping on that sofa. I'm a big man. Far too big for a sofa. I never even did that in my teenage years.'

'You never slept rough?'

'Never. But we're getting off topic here. We will have to be a bit more proactive. I admit, I've been at fault here…' Yes, he had. He had preferred to enjoy the atmosphere in the house, his mother's delight with his latest conquest, so different from her reactions to the few women she had met over the years. Lazy. He had been lazy. 'Tomorrow, we stage an argument. It shouldn't be too difficult. We have precious little in common.' He shrugged with the usual graceful nonchalance that Milly found so seductive.

Milly drank some of the white wine that had found itself into the oversized glass in front of her. She had hardly been aware of a waiter pouring from a bottle.

'If we have so little in common,' she mocked, 'then how is it that we haven't been at each other's throats by now?'

Lucas flushed. It was a good question. 'It's called the route of least resistance. When my mother has been around, it has been all too easy to let her see what she has wanted to see, but I have a life to get on with. I can't afford to spend much more time here. Naturally, I will commute on weekends, but I need to be back in the saddle. I need to return to London. As do you. So that you can make good on the bargain you struck with me. Have you told your landlord that you will no longer be needing his flat? Or house? Or wherever it is you live?'

'House. I've already told you that.'

'My short-term memory can be occasionally short.' The house she had shared with her so-called good friend. Of course he remembered! He remembered everything, every little detail. Too much.

'And, no, I haven't told my landlord yet. I can email him in the morning but you have to give me your word that you won't renege on our agreement. I don't want to find myself without a roof over my head.'

'You did as you were asked. Naturally I will keep my end of the bargain.'

He was barely aware of ordering another bottle and, by the time they had finished eating, they were two bottles down and were making inroads into a third.

'And what do you think our staged argument should be about?' After a brief lull in hostilities, Milly picked up the thread of what they had been discussing earlier. The meal was finished, the bill paid; when she stood up, she had to focus, *really focus,* to stop herself from teetering on her unfamiliar heels.

He reached out to steady her and his hand remained there at her waist.

'You've had too much to drink,' Lucas murmured.

'Maybe we could weave *that* in. Maybe you could turn me into an alcoholic.'

'My mother would never buy it.'

'Because I'm such a *boring* girl-next-door type?'

'Where did *that* come from?' He stopped dead in his tracks and spun her to face him. Of their own volition, his fingers sifted through her hair and brushed her cheek.

Milly was transfixed by that gesture. He was staring down at her and she experienced a weird, drowning feeling. He was right. She'd drunk too much. She couldn't peel her eyes away from his handsome face.

'You should stop looking at me like that,' Lucas said huskily and Milly half-closed her eyes.

'Like what?' she breathed.

'Boring girl-next-door types don't look at men the way you're looking at me…'

Milly reached out and tentatively touched his cheek, and was blown away when she realised that that was what she had been longing to do since…*for ever.* She let her hand linger there, feeling the roughened stubble on his chin, while her heart carried on beating like a sledgehammer inside her.

'No,' Lucas said shakily. 'Come on. Carlos is waiting.'

And he meant it. However tempting she might be, he wasn't going to make love to her. No way. The prospect enticed and, yes, *frightened* him in equal measure. It was an unfamiliar feeling. It disturbed and unsteadied him. It smacked of a loss of control.

'I'm going to put you to bed as soon as we're back.' He was dismayed when she nodded and nestled against his arm. She smelled floral, clean, *young*.

'So, tell me what vices you're going to give me,' Milly encouraged, at once sleepy and yet never so wide awake. She felt alive to everything: to the scent of him; to the rough feel of the linen jacket he had flung on before leaving the house; to the way his chest rose and fell as he breathed. 'I've always thought it must be nice to have a few vices.'

Lucas wasn't doing much thinking at all. He cleared his throat, shifted, failed to budge her...knew that he didn't want to anyway, not really. The key thing was that he wasn't going to make a move on her.

'Not a cry I've often heard,' he remarked drily.

'I guess you heard what I was telling your mother about Robbie...having a crush on him. He was so cool when he was young.'

'And now less so,' Lucas reminded her shortly. 'A loser, in fact.'

'I bet you think that everyone's a loser compared to you,' Milly murmured, wriggling so that she could tilt her head and look him directly in the eye.

Her breath caught in her throat and her racing heart slowed, along with time, which seemed to stand still altogether.

Her kiss took him by surprise, reaching up on tiptoe as she did, and it was so sweetly, disarmingly innocent; the gentle, tentative probing of her cool tongue a breathless, feathery flutter against his lips..

He shuddered and stifled a groan. 'This isn't part of the deal,' he muttered unsteadily.

'I know. But remember those vices I wished I had? One of them was to just...*let go*, not take guys so *seriously*...' She traced the outline of his jaw, could sense him wanting more against his will and that filled her with a heady sense of power. When he pressed a button so that opaque glass separated them from Carlos, she smiled.

So the big break-up was going to start tomorrow. And then, in a heartbeat, she would be back in London, back to reality… But, right now, *this* was her reality and why shouldn't she grab it with both hands? If he pushed her away and stormed off in revulsion, then so be it, but deep inside she sensed that he wouldn't do that.

'You see them and you what…? Want to marry them?'

'I see them and I start wondering how they would fit in on a long-term basis.' Which was pretty badly in every case thus far, few though those cases had been. 'Sort of, "hi, how are you? What are your thoughts on big families…?"' She felt him shudder and laughed. 'I know. You're horrified. I bet you'd run a mile if a woman asked you a question like that. I mean, you gave your heart away and you got burned, right? So you're not up to giving it away again.'

'You got that right but, word to the wise, don't mention that particular bone of contention to my mother. She might not quite see my side of the story.'

'Oh, I won't mention anything that might give her the wrong idea about us,' Milly said with a hitch in her voice. She didn't want to think about going. Not right at this moment.

What she wanted…

She covered his big hand with her much smaller one and guided it to her breast, and she felt him slip a little lower in the seat.

'Hell, Milly! No. You…don't know what you're doing…' But he kept his hand there, felt the rounded fullness of her breast, and wanted to do so much more that it was a physical ache. His erection was so hard that he could barely move.

'I *do* know what I'm doing. For the first time in my

whole life, I know what I'm doing.' Her voice was insistent as she unbuttoned the top two pearl buttons of the dress, allowing him more access to her and loving, absolutely *loving,* the way he was making her feel. 'I'll be gone in a few days and I won't be seeing you again… And…you make me feel…'

'How do I make you feel, Milly?' *More than a handful.* She was well endowed; if Carlos hadn't been in the front seat, driving them slowly with an impeccable lack of interest in the goings on behind him, he would have taken her right here in the car.

'Curious,' she confessed with the honesty that was so much a part and parcel of her personality. 'You make me feel curious.'

CHAPTER NINE

THE KING-SIZE BED that had been her hiding place for nearly two weeks seemed suddenly to have expanded until now she felt as though it was consuming all the space in the room. It was the only thing she could see.

Milly's body was on fire. 'Sexually daring and adventurous' were not descriptions that could ever have been applied to her. The truth was that she had never felt particularly bothered by her lack of experience in this field. She had kissed a few guys and had been content enough to leave it right there. Now, though, her head was filled with possibilities.

'This…isn't a good idea.' Common sense half-heartedly tried to prevail but Lucas recognised it for what it was: a flimsy attempt to hold off something that felt inevitable. He had already dumped his jacket downstairs and his fingers were hooked under the polo shirt, ready to yank it over his head. He was breathing fast as he stared at her, not trusting himself to get any closer, because that flimsy attempt at common sense wouldn't stand a chance.

'Why not?' Milly asked with reckless abandon. She took a couple of steps towards him.

They hadn't switched on the light, and the bedroom was bathed in pale moonlit rays sifting through the big windows. His beautiful face was a mix of shadows and angles, his eyes glittering as he watched her nervous progress.

He felt nervous, as well. Unbelievable.

'Don't you fancy me at all?' she asked, placing the palm of her hand on his chest and feeling the steady beating of his heart underneath it.

'What sort of stupid question is that?' Lucas returned roughly. He covered her hand with his and guided it to the bulging hardness of his erection pushing against the zip of his jeans.

Milly shivered, unbelievably turned on. So turned on that she forgot to be scared that this was going to be her *first time*. With trembling fingers, she hitched down the zip and heard his sharp, indrawn breath with a jab of pure satisfaction.

She had taken a chance, had been prepared to stomach his rejection because her own shameless craving felt like something requiring satisfaction before she packed her bags and walked away. The feel of his arousal was proof that he wanted her, too, even if he didn't think it was a good idea.

With a growl of impatience, Lucas pulled off the polo shirt, revealing a bronzed, muscular body that was as exquisite and as perfect as the rest of him. Any wonder she had dumped all her reservations? Breathing shallow, she ran her fingers lightly over his torso, pausing to circle the tight, brown nipples.

'We're supposed to be lovers…' She looked up at him with a wry smile. 'Aren't we?'

'How is it that you haven't felt this pressing need to touch me before?'

'Who says I haven't?'

Lucas's smile was triumphant. Common sense flew

through the window. He began unbuttoning the tiny pearl buttons, taking his time, until the top half of the dress was gaping, allowing him to see tantalising glimpses of her soft breasts.

'You weren't wearing a bra,' he murmured huskily. 'That was the first thing I noticed when I saw you this evening.'

'I had no idea you even noticed what I was wearing, considering you didn't say anything.'

'The sight left me speechless.'

Milly smiled. 'Speechless in a good way?'

'Speechless in a way that made me want to do what I'm about to do now.' He hooked his fingers under the spaghetti straps of the dress and slowly pulled himself down until he was feasting his eyes on the proud jut of her breasts.

Milly stood absolutely still, which was the only way she could think of to restrain herself from pulling the dress back into position. She didn't want to think of all the lovely bodies he had looked at before because she was not built like one of them.

'Don't say anything.'

'Not hard. I find…' He circled one rosy nipple with his finger and felt her shudder. 'I find myself without words…'

'I'm not tall and skinny. I'm short and well-endowed… Sorry.'

Lucas looked at her in genuine amazement at her self-denigration. 'I've never heard anything so ridiculous in all my life.'

'Thank you for that.' Romantic fool she might be but she could also be as realistic as he assumed she was not, and she was realistic enough to know that what he saw was the novelty of a differently shaped body and a differently fashioned personality from those to which he was accustomed. But the moment would be lost if she embarked on that sort of conversation. It was a topic best left alone.

She walked shakily towards the bed and seconds later he joined her, tossing the condom he had sourced onto the small bedside table.

'Take off the dress,' he commanded. 'No, just let it fall open… Yes, like that. I want to see you…' He straddled her prone body and just watched, savouring the tight buds of her nipples. He removed his jeans and enjoyed the way her eyes skittered away from his pulsing erection before looking once again. 'Feel free to touch.' He barely recognised his voice.

Milly gulped and tentatively tugged down the boxers. He was impressive in his girth, his erection as big, as powerful and as striking as he was. She took it in her hand and instinct took over. At first, she kept her eyes half-closed, but then opened them and looked at the shiny head in her hand then, growing braver, she sat up and took him into her mouth.

She tasted him and felt him shudder, move and arch back. His fingers had coiled in her long hair. The salty taste of him was an aphrodisiac, sending waves of pleasure and yearning through her in equal measure.

She moaned when he pushed her back. Her underwear was wet, her own arousal soaking through the cotton, and she wriggled and kicked herself free of it, parting her legs in an attempt to cool between them.

'You're burning up for me.' Lucas slipped exploring fingers into her and her breath caught in her throat as he found her clitoris and began rubbing it, gentle, persistent strokes that made her arch her body up, transported like she had never been before in her life.

She didn't want to come. Not like this. She pulled him to her and kissed him and Lord…it was beautiful. It was a kiss meant to be lost in. His tongue against hers was gentle and demanding at the same time. She could taste the essence of the guy who wanted to move slowly and yet was desperate to sate his hunger. His steel shaft brushed against her and she opened her legs a little wider so that she could feel its hardness against the parted, delicate folds. She moaned softly into his mouth, quivering when his erection pressed against her clitoris, threatening to push her over the edge.

She broke apart and captured his face between her hands. 'There's something I should tell you.'

'Now isn't the time for sharing confidences,' Lucas breathed shakily. He pinned her arms above her head and ordered her to keep them there.

Then he lowered his head to taste her succulent nipples, circling first one then the other with his mouth, drawing them deeply in then teasing the stiffened bud with his tongue.

Milly couldn't bear it. It was beyond pleasurable. It was also a completely new experience. She wanted to tell him that she was a virgin. He deserved to know, didn't he? Or else he might expect her to…be like all his other women. She wasn't sure what that meant, exactly, but she thought that creative gymnastics might be involved.

She half-opened her mouth and a gasp of pure pleasure came out instead of the haltering admission she had been formulating.

He was licking her nipple, watching her, enjoying the hectic colour in her cheeks, enjoying the way she couldn't keep still, all her little soft moans and whimpers.

Her full breasts jiggled as she writhed under him and he was driven to capture her other nipple, suckling on it until the moans became husky and uncontrolled.

He'd never felt the need to rush his love-making. Sex was an art form and pleasure had to be given and taken in equal measure. He was a master of taking things slowly, of the languorous intimate exploration, but right now it required a great deal of self-control not to grab the condom on the bedside table, stick it on and just...*take her.* Where his skinny supermodels were all sharp angles and jutting hip bones, Milly was soft, silky smooth and sensually rounded.

He curved his hand along her side, mouth still firmly clamped on her breast, then over the gentle swell of her stomach to slip between her legs, although once there he simply smoothed her inner thigh. His knuckles brushed the soft down of her pubic hair, and he itched to delve deeper, but all in good time.

Very slowly...and trying hard to douse his raging libido by concentrating on something, anything, other than the sex bomb squirming under him...he licked a trail along her stomach, starting from underneath her heavy breasts and working all the way down to her belly button.

He tipped his tongue into the sensitive indentation and felt the whoosh of her breath as she inhaled sharply. She had pressed her legs together and he gently but firmly eased them apart in preparation of tasting her but she tugged him by his hair and he glanced up to meet her feverish eyes.

'What are you doing?' Milly whispered, yearning for his mouth to touch her in her most private part, yet horrified at this outrageous show of intimacy.

'Nothing while you're pulling my hair out.'

'It's just that…'

'Don't tell me that no one has ever tasted you… there…' Could his libido get any more out of control? he wondered.

'I…' Confession time—but her vocal cords protested at ruining the moment and what difference would it make anyway? She still wanted him, wanted *this*.

Lucas slanted a bone-melting smile at her and her fingers slackened their grip. She fell back, eyes closed, cautiously opened her legs then sucked in deeply and held her breath as his tongue began to tease her open, flicking over the stiffened nub of her clitoris. She exhaled but had to breath in quickly again because sensations were running rampant through her.

She was burning up all over and panting. No part of her could keep still under the force of the fire spreading through her body, wafting through her in waves, making her arch up against his mouth, and there he kept her by placing his hands firmly under her butt.

He brought her close, so close that she wanted to cry out, then pulled back, teasing her body in a way that had her breathless and shamefully pleading for him to enter her.

She felt rather than saw him fumble for the condom he had earlier fished out. She watched, cheeks hot, as he expertly slipped it on, never taking his eyes off her face. She felt that she should have done more—clambered over him, perhaps, enticed him with the promise of new, acrobatic positions—but she dismissed that jag of insecurity. The hunger blazing in his dark eyes left no room for her to doubt that he was as turned on as she was.

He nudged the thick head of his arousal into her, and she tensed and stifled a little yelp as he inserted more of his tremendous girth into her, plunging deep and hard. She stiffened, eyes wide and panicked, and he stopped as realisation dawned.

'Tell me you're not a virgin,' he gasped, his whole body so still that it sent a ripple of alarm racing through her.

'You said that this was no time for confiding.' Milly pulled him down to her, raising herself slightly so that she could kiss him.

'Oh, Milly of the not-red hair, I'll take my time… I'll be gentle…'

He did, teasing her with his arousal, nudging it slowly in, withdrawing it, enticing her until her little whimpers became pleading moans. It was agony. But there was no way that he was going to hurt her, no way that she would ever think back to this night as anything but utterly memorable. Why that meant so much to him was something he shoved away.

She was wet and slippery as he eased himself deeper, taking his time as he had promised, until she was crying out for him to take her and take her *now*.

With a groan, Lucas thrust deep into her, and after the first sharp shock of his entry her body settled around him, responding to his deep, fierce thrusts, and the orgasm she had come so close to having when his mouth had been exploring her built into something wild and unstoppable.

She cried out and he placed a hand gently over her mouth, lifting his hand and grinning, then kissing her and coming as his mouth was still on hers, tasting her as his big body shuddered.

Spent, he backtracked and registered what she had confessed earlier.

'You're a virgin.' He eased himself off her and

flopped onto his side then immediately propped himself on one elbow to stare at her.

And this was why he had stayed away. Not that he'd known that, but still, he'd known enough: had known that she wasn't tough like the women he dated; had known that she was one of life's romantics; had known that she was still in a vulnerable place. That she was a virgin took a stupid situation and threatened to turn it into a very messy one.

But, hell, the sex had been good.

A virgin. He'd never placed any value on that particular virtue at all but now he wanted to take her all over again, show her things she had never experienced before, teach her, make love to her with all the gentle command at his disposal.

None of it made sense but he couldn't fight the realisation. Since when had he become a he-man bore who got a chauvinistic kick out of bedding virgins? What next? Belting out a Tarzan yell and looking for a vine to swing on?

But he couldn't contain a deep sense of mystifying satisfaction.

'You should have told me.'

'I was going to. Does it matter?'

'What I don't understand is *why*?'

'I don't want to talk about this.' Milly rolled onto her back and stared up at the ceiling. This had been the most wonderful experience in her entire life. Nothing had prepared her for all the amazing sensations that had bombarded her entire body; nothing. And yet all he could take away from it was the fact that she hadn't told him that he was her first.

Lucas propped himself up, invading her space so that she was forced to look at him. 'I apologise if I wasn't up to your high standards,' she managed to choke out and his eyebrows shot up.

'What the heck's going through your head, Milly?'

'What do you think?' She drew in a deep breath and said what was on her mind. 'We've just made love, and I know that it's probably not a big deal for you, but the only thing you seem to care about is the fact that I've never done this before. Is it because you're... I know those women you dated...supermodels...'

'Don't *ever* run yourself down to me, Milly. Ever. That has nothing to do with...anything.' He sighed his frustration. Even the way she *looked* at things was different. Why the instant rush to denigrate herself? In so many areas she was the most outspoken, cheerful and upbeat woman he had ever met...and yet there was an insecurity there that was reflected in the wounded, accusing eyes looking at him.

He had a moment of disturbing tenderness that threw him for a few seconds and then he rationalised that it was because he didn't usually do this, didn't usually have cosy conversations with women after sex. But naturally Milly would want to have that conversation because this had been her first time and by nature she was confiding and talkative. Of course she wasn't going to keep quiet and uncomplaining when he rose from the bed to have a shower and check his emails.

'I expressed puzzlement that you were still a virgin because you're so damned hot, Milly.'

She allowed her hurt to dissipate a little. 'I'm not.'

'Are we going to waste time playing the "no, I'm not—oh yes, you are" game?' He brushed a lock of hair from her cheek and hardened at the thought of taking her again.

Milly was tempted to tell him that she quite liked the

idea of that game. 'I practically threw myself at you. Most men would take what was on offer even if they didn't fancy it.'

'I'm not most men and we seem to be coming back to the fishing for compliments game. I fancied you the minute I laid eyes on you at my ski lodge.'

'You did?' Now she *definitely* wanted to hear more.

'And now here we are, in bed together, and trust me—I enjoyed every second of the experience. In fact, if I didn't think you were sore, I would repeat it right now all over again...' He cupped her with his hand and her eyelids fluttered. 'Why me?'

'Sorry?' Milly dragged her addled brain into some sort of functioning order and frowned.

'You're hopelessly romantic...'

'Not *hopelessly.*'

'Romantic enough for me to wonder why you would choose your first experience to be with me, under these circumstances. I'm curious as to why you didn't sleep with the man you presumed you were going to marry but you were happy to hop in the sack with a guy you definitely won't be ending up with.'

'I haven't sat down and analysed it but...I guess, maybe, I just needed...'

'A tonic? A pick-me-up? And I happened to be the nearest suitable medication to hand? Wasn't the ex man enough to entice you into bed?'

'The ex didn't fancy me,' Milly said bluntly. 'So he didn't put much effort into trying.'

'And you didn't bother to try either.'

'I...' *I was never the sort of girl to make the first move.* Yet she had made the first move with Lucas, hadn't she? Was it because she'd had nothing to lose?

Or was it because she had never grasped the full meaning of lust until she'd met him?

'I suppose I was waiting for the big night.' In love with the thought of being in love, but she'd never fancied Robbie. Lucas had shown her that; lust and love were two separate things, miles apart. She stared at his lean, dark face for a few disorientated seconds. 'You're right. Stupidly romantic. This is real life. Maybe subconsciously that's what I wanted, to connect with real life…'

'A man could be hurt.'

'I can't picture you ever being hurt. I mean, so hurt that you wanted to cry.'

'Oh, Milly. The things you come out with. So, ironically, we're lovers for real but still on course for self-destruction…' He brushed his fingers over her nipple, which hardened in fast response. 'Shall we think about how we do that while we rediscover each other again…? Or maybe we'll have to do the thinking *after* the rediscovery has finished…because I guarantee you won't be thinking when we're making love…'

Lucas pushed himself away from his desk and restively strolled towards the bank of windows that overlooked the city. He was back in London, back in his towering office, back in the thick of it. This was his reality. The two-and-a-half weeks spent with his mother playing Romeo to Milly's Juliet had been a mirage, flimsy and insubstantial, easily blown away after a fortnight. Then, business as usual.

So what the heck had happened?

He raked fingers through his hair frustratedly and silently cursed himself for letting things get out of hand. It was a mess. They had returned to London, his mother none the wiser that their relationship, whilst it had become physical, was just a sham. Marriage was not on the cards. *Longevity* was not on the cards.

But that was nearly two months ago and now…

Entrenched. And in a place from which an exit had to be made. Accustomed as he was to making the most of a bad situation, Lucas decided that this was something from which a positive could be drawn. Perhaps it had been foolish to imagine that he could take Milly to Spain and, in the space of a mere week or two, manage to convince his very astute mother that their brief romance was drawing to its sad but inevitable close.

Wasn't it better this way? The relationship had lasted long enough for its demise to be more credible. They had got to know one another and unfortunately familiarity had bred contempt. His mother would not have witnessed the decline in their relations. It would be easy to report back that they were no longer an item. Disappointment all round, but that was life.

He prowled restlessly through his vast office. It was late. He was probably the last man standing in the office. Milly, now settled into her new apartment and her new job, was having an evening out with her new colleagues. A drink at some pub somewhere with a meal to follow.

What colleagues?

Lucas impatiently pushed away any line of pointless speculation. It was good that she was making lots of friends. So what if some of them were men? It was to be expected. She had smartened up her act when it came to her dress code. He had, she had told him more than once, given her confidence in the way she looked, in her body. She had had a ritual getting rid of most of her old clothes, which, much to his amusement, she had insisted in showing him piece by deplorable piece. He had never seen such a vast collection of shapeless items of clothing in one place in his life before. Then she had dragged him out shopping.

He gritted his teeth at the thought of some guy seeing her in some of the stuff they had bought together. The red dress with the plunging back; the tight black jeans; hell, some of the sexy underwear...

He only had himself to blame for the situation he now found himself in. He had known from the very beginning that she was vulnerable. He had known that she was the sort of romantic who got lost in house and garden magazines and gazed longingly into the windows of bridal shops. She had a strong nesting instinct and was a home-maker by nature. She had loved cooking for him and he, who had never allowed any woman the privilege of cosy home-cooked meals in his kitchens, had found himself trying out new recipes and working while she sat cross-legged next to him, watching rubbish on television.

Was it any wonder that she had fallen in love with him? Was it any wonder that she had risen to the futile challenge of trying to make him see that his teenage error of judgement was just a little something that 'true love' could overcome?

Before she had even told him, he had *known*. She wasn't good when it came to hiding things. She wore her heart on her sleeve, and he had seen it in her eyes but had chosen to ignore it because he enjoyed her company and the sex was better than brilliant.

But he wasn't going to marry her and just the thought of being the object of her love, just the memory of those hopeful, trusting, *adoring* eyes on him, filled him with a sense of claustrophobia.

Love was for fools. He had learnt that the tough way. She knew that and if she had chosen to ignore it, then, *hell*!

The long and short of it was that he had taken his eye off the ball…and now…

He made his mind up, grabbed his jacket and left the office before he had time for any weakness to seep in.

He, of course, had a key to the apartment. It *was* his, after all; why wouldn't he? On a couple of occasions, he had left work early and headed straight there, letting himself in and working until she returned.

In a short space of time, she had made inroads into the decor. The perfectly cool, bland apartment now bore just the sort of homey touches that should have warned him that she was settling into it, just as she was settling into him.

Pictures on the mantelpiece. Scraps of paper with handy recipe titbits pinned to the stainless steel American-style fridge-freezer with jokey magnets. Lots of flowers because, she told him, it had always been her grandmother's habit to fill the rooms with things from outside. Good Feng Shui, apparently. He had laughed and drily told her that he had lived quite happily without such touches in his own place. She had suggested some kind of water feature; he had firmly squashed that idea, but he suspected that its absence was only short lived.

He had to wait for over an hour and a half before he heard the turn of the key in the door and, in that hour and a half, his mind had been everywhere but on work. For once, the joys of deal making had failed in its duty to distract him.

'Where've you been?' was his opening question as

she entered the sitting room and Milly started, then smiled as her breathing returned to normal.

He had been on her mind all evening. So she had told him, just blurted it out; she hadn't been able to help herself. She had fallen in love with him and it had been just too big a deal for her to keep inside. She didn't even know when the process had begun. Maybe the seeds had been sown in Spain, when she had glimpsed sides of him that were so curiously appealing. Certainly, she now knew that her fate had been sealed by the time they had fallen into bed together that first time and she had sunk deeper and deeper the longer she had spent with him.

It was crazy, she had known that, but love was crazy, wasn't it? It wasn't something you could explain on a sheet of A4 paper, like a maths problem with a solution. If love made sense, she would never have fallen in love with Lucas. But she had. And, the minute she had told him, she had wished that she could yank the words back into her mouth and swallow them down. He had gone perfectly still, hadn't replied, and when he *had* spoken it was as though he had chosen to ignore what she had said.

And his eyes were grave now as she tentatively walked towards him.

'We need to talk.'

'Why?' Milly smiled quickly. 'You always tell me that there are far better things to do than talk.'

'But, first, where have you been?' That question hadn't been on the agenda.

'I told you, Lucas, that I was going out with some people from work.'

Lucas scowled and tried not to let his imagination run away with thoughts of who those people were. She looked bloody amazing. Just the right side of tousled, her red hair trailing down her back, her tight jeans showing off every succulent inch of her body, as did the clingy long-sleeved top. The fact that she was wearing a pair of flat sneakers did nothing to detract from the look and he angrily felt himself harden in automatic response.

He dismissively waved aside her explanation just in case she thought that a detour down that road was going to happen.

'What's going on, Lucas?' As if she didn't know. One sign of love and he was getting ready to bolt. Things were just fine as long as they were having sex. The charade was well in place then! But she had crossed a line; she had forgotten what he had told her about not getting involved and had committed the mortal sin of not only disobeying the edict, but of telling him that she had.

'I think you know. And sit down; stop hovering.'

'I'm not sorry I said what I said,' Milly imparted with just the sort of driven honesty that he felt had landed them in this mess. 'And I never said that I was asking you to love me back.' *But she was.*

'This is no longer a working proposition.' He was somehow angry and bewildered as to how it was that these seemed to be the hardest words ever to have left his mouth. He had known that it was going to end sooner or later. So why did each syllable feel like broken glass? Maybe it was because he hadn't been the one to determine the timing of the end. He had been pushed into it because unforeseen circumstances had forced his hand. That made sense. He, of all men, did not like having his hand forced.

Milly opened her mouth but nothing emerged. She stared at him, wide-eyed, not daring to speak in case she started doing something really humiliating…like pleading and begging. Because, for the life of her, she couldn't envisage life without him.

Stupid Robbie and her broken engagement had been a walk in the park in comparison. This was the real thing. This was love, and hearing him tell her that their relationship was over was like staring down the barrel of a gun and waiting for the trigger to be pulled.

Did she regret her honesty? No. Was she going to compound her horror and dismay by really pushing the boat out and bursting into tears? Absolutely not!

'I get it,' she told him quietly. 'And I agree.'

CHAPTER TEN

A WEEK AND a half later, Milly could still scarcely believe that she had shown such fortitude in the face of the groundswell of misery that had been gathering at her feet.

So she had hung on to her pride, but at what cost? He was on her mind twenty-four-seven. She thought of him when she was working, when she was relaxing, and she dreamed of him when she was asleep.

He hadn't argued with her when she had conceded defeat. He had wanted out and she hadn't fought to bar him from the exit he was desperate to take. But he had been as quick to rush through the open door as she might have expected. He had continued the conversation: had told her in a cool, detached voice that he had never been in it for the long term; that he had warned her that commitment was off limits for him; that she should have known that after everything he had told her. His voice had been thick with accusation.

She had agreed with him.

'Off the cards and especially with someone like me,' she had obliged him by pointing out. All the time, her heart had been beating so hard and so fast that her breathing was short and raspy.

'With anyone. I'm not interested in a long-term relationship and I should never have allowed myself to be swept into something with a woman who was vulnerable and in search of a life partner.'

'I may have been vulnerable but I was *not* in search of a life partner! And I may have fallen in love with you, but has it occurred to you that I'm not as ditzy as you think I am? Has it occurred to you that I *know* we're not suited?'

Of course it hadn't occurred to him.

'We're different people from different backgrounds,' she had persisted. 'And that might not make a difference, but we're also like oil and water. You're darkness to my light. I'm not suspicious and distrusting of everyone; I like giving people chances. And I know you think I'm naive and stupid because I should have learned from Robbie and what happened but maybe, just maybe, that makes me a happier person than you, Lucas! You had one crappy experience and you've let it dictate the rest of your life! How does that make sense?'

'So you're prepared to carry on as we are with no expectations?' he had mocked. 'You're fine if I tell you that I'm more than happy to take you to my bed but that's all there is to it?'

Naturally she wouldn't have been fine with that and her brief hesitation had given him all the answer he had needed.

But what if she *had* agreed? What if she had buried her feelings under the sort of hard veneer that he would have been able to deal with? What if she had taken up his proposition and shut away the side of her that had wanted more, that would always want more? Would that have been a better decision than the one she had made? She wouldn't have spent the past week and a half thinking about him whilst staring at the walls of his apartment and thinking that she would have to move out sooner rather than later.

She almost, but didn't quite, regretted that she hadn't thrown his stupid job and his stupid free apartment right back in his face but common sense had thankfully kicked in because she would have been in an even worse position than she was now. She would have been hurting emotionally, and positively haemorrhaging financially, because a cursory glimpse at the ads for jobs in the catering industry had told her that there were no jobs to speak of. She would have been on the first train back to her grandmother, and there would have been no jobs there either, so she would have ended up doing something and nothing just to make ends meet.

It had left a sour taste in her mouth because the last thing she had wanted to do was to accept the terms and conditions of the proposal that had so roundly backfired in her face. But sometimes pride just had to take a back seat, and she was very glad that it had, because she loved her job and loved living in the heart of London, such a far cry from her former digs.

Her friends had all been mightily impressed as well, although she had omitted to tell them the details of how she had landed up where she had.

She had simply said that she had been lucky enough to have found herself in the company of a guy who had felt sorry enough for her to have lent her a helping hand. It was bad luck to have found herself at the ski chalet without the job she had anticipated, but it had been extremely good luck to have found herself there in the company of the guy who actually owned the ski chalet, along with a whole load of other stuff; a guy who had heard her unfortunate story and had been kind enough to lend a helping hand.

Ha. She had nearly choked when she had expanded on his *kindness*. She had turned him into a benevolent, avuncular, father-figure type, which couldn't have been further from the truth!

If they had been a little curious as to why she had suddenly decided to become the stay-at-home type who no longer needed to talk incessantly about her misfortunes, they had not said anything, and she knew they figured that she was just experiencing the aftershocks of what had happened with Robbie.

In time, she would confess all, but right now she needed time out from…*everyone.*

She had just showered and climbed into a pair of baggy joggers and an even baggier T-shirt—because she had lost the desire to wear tight and sexy clothes now that she was back to being on her own—when she heard the ring of the doorbell, and she froze, because there could be only one person who would ring that doorbell, having got past Eddy, the porter who manned the desk downstairs.

Lucas.

He had a key to the apartment, which made sense bearing in mind it belonged to him, but he always used the doorbell, only letting himself in if he knew that she wasn't going to be in.

Her mouth went dry and she gulped in deep breaths because the thought of seeing him again filled her with pleasure and trepidation at the same time.

In the length of time it took her to traverse the wooden floor from sitting room to door, she had dissected, dismissed and re-dissected a hundred possible reasons for this unexpected visit.

In the starring role on her wish list was the tiny ray of hope that he had miraculously decided that they were suited after all, that he had made a terrible mistake. Or even, she was ashamed to concede, that he had missed her and would she climb back into bed with him? She would say no, she was pretty sure of that, but it would do her a power of good just to think that he, in some small way, missed her as much as she was desperately missing him.

Her heart was preparing to soar and she had to school her features into just the right level of indifference as she pulled open the door.

'My dear!'

'Antonia…' Milly forced a smile but she was taken aback to find his mother on the doorstep. She hadn't spoken to Antonia since the split, and she felt guilty now about that, because they had developed a strong bond in the short time they had been in each other's company. 'I…eh…have been meaning to get in touch with you…'

'You look a little peaky, my dear.'

'Please, come inside. I… What brings you to London? I didn't think that you would be okay to travel overseas…just yet. Can I offer you something? Tea or coffee?'

'I thought I might surprise my son with a visit,' Antonia confided. 'And a cup of coffee would be lovely, my dear. Decaf, if you have it. Caffeine any time after six in the evening ruins my sleeping patterns.'

'That reminds me: well, I guess you've come… I would have called…' *To further compound your disappointment by filling in all the gaps Lucas might have left in the saga of why we had broken up? Added to the story of personality clashes, simmering rows and different hopes and dreams?*

'It's even nicer seeing you face to face, Milly, my

dear. I've missed having you there at the house. It felt rather empty and quiet after you and Lucas left. Of course, I was in tremendous spirits, but nevertheless… How quickly we become accustomed to having pleasant company around us.'

Milly could feel her face getting redder and redder and her body hotter and hotter.

'Well, you look amazing,' she said truthfully, *even though the tremendous spirits may have taken a recent battering.*

'I feel it. I guess I'm just buoyed up by Lucas's turnaround.'

'His turnaround…?'

'Finally coming to his senses and seeing the value of settling down.'

For a confusing few seconds, Milly was appalled at the question that had instantly sprung into her head: *Who* was he planning to settle down with? How fast could one man move when it came to women?

'So—and I know I'm being an interfering old witch here—but I came over so that I could sit you both down together and find out when I can start looking forward to the big day…'

'*The big day,* Lucas…and I'm quoting here. So *what* in heck's name is going on?'

Milly had finally managed to get hold of Lucas, who was personally protected from hassle with anyone he might not wish to talk to by an army of people in charge of security checks. She actually had his direct line but, the second she had been redirected, she had had to engage in the usual barrage of questions from his guard dogs.

She was in a filthy temper by the time she actually

heard his dark drawl at the other end of the line, which was possibly why her stomach didn't instantly go into nervous knots.

For the first time since he had walked out, Lucas felt alive at the sound of her voice and that, in itself, was bloody infuriating.

'I have no idea what you're going on about, Milly. You can't commence a conversation in mid-sentence and expect me to instantly be clued up.'

'You *know* what I'm talking about! Guess who I just had a visit from?'

'Can't think. No time for guessing games.'

'Your *mother*!'

Lucas sat up and digested this piece of information. 'My mother…' he said slowly.

'Strangely,' Milly all but shrieked down the end of the line, 'she seems to be under the impression that we're still an item!'

'Where are you?'

'Where do you think I am, Lucas?'

'How would I know?' he answered with silky smoothness. 'It's after seven on a Friday evening and you're a single woman…'

'I'm at home.' How could he think that she would physically be able to go clubbing when she was in love with him? Or was he just judging her the way he judged himself? He would have no problem doing that. If he possessed a heart instead of a lump of cold where a heart should be…

'I'm on my way.'

Milly fought the temptation to get a little more dolled up than she was. Maybe swop the baggy jogging bottoms, which she knew he loathed, for something a little more attractive. He could take her as he found her, she decided. He could explain why his mother was still in the dark and then he could be on his way.

She was as cool as a cucumber until the doorbell went half an hour later and there he was. All dark, tall and broodingly, sinfully gorgeous. Just the right side of dishevelled with the sleeves of his white shirt rolled to the elbows and his jacket slung over one shoulder. A sight for sore eyes and she just wanted to stand there and stare.

'So…' She pulled open the door and stepped away from him, not trusting herself. 'Mind explaining…?'

Lucas couldn't peel his eyes away from her. She was wearing just the sort of outfit he had always teased that she needed to wean herself away from. It hid every delectable curve, and yet she was still so enticing, still so damned *sexy*.

He'd missed her. It was as simple as that. He hadn't been able to focus, had lost interest in deals that should have netted all of his undivided attention, could not even be bothered to rifle through his little black book for other women. And he had told his mother nothing because…

'I need a drink. Something stronger than a cup of tea.'

'You *need a drink*? This isn't a social call, Lucas.' Milly finally looked at him and her treacherous eyes skittered away. She clasped her arms around her body, hugging herself.

'No. It's not.' He headed straight for the kitchen, directly to the cupboard where he knew she kept a practically full bottle of whisky, and he poured himself a hefty glass, keenly aware that she had padded in behind him. He imagined her arms were still folded and her full mouth would be pursed in a moue of frustration.

She loved him. She *had* loved him. Did she still?

'I intended to tell her...'

'But somehow you didn't manage to get round to it? Even though you speak to her every other day? That titbit just managed to *get lost* amidst the chit chat?'

'No.'

'Okay...' She looked at him hesitantly, picking up vibes which, for once, he wasn't bothering to hide. He had sat down at the kitchen table and was nursing his drink, not looking at her—again, a little weird, because it smacked of the sort of indecision not associated with him. She felt in need of a stiff drink as well but instead made do with a glass of juice from the fridge before sitting opposite him at the chrome-and-glass table.

'I could have told her but...I needed time.'

'Time for what?'

'Time to come to terms with the fact that we were really no longer an item.' He looked at her with serious intent and swallowed a mouthful of the whisky, not taking his eyes from her flushed face. 'I thought...when you told me that you loved me...'

'I don't want to go there.'

'We don't have a choice.'

'We do!' she cried. 'I said what I said and there's no point going over it!'

'I've never believed in love.'

'I told you—I get that.'

'You don't. You don't because, as you said, I let one crappy experience dictate my future where you, my optimistic Milly, would never have allowed that to happen. So, no, you didn't understand. Not really.'

He shot her a crooked, hesitant smile.

'Do you know that you were the first person I ever told about Betina and my youthful error of judgement?

And I knew that every time you raised the subject, which was often, you were trying to come to terms with the way I thought, because it was so unlike the way *you* would think. I should have been enraged at having that one confidence thrown back in my face time and again. I wasn't.'

He looked at his glass, circled the rim with his finger.

'We're all creatures of habit to some extent. My habit lay in the way I thought, the way I conditioned myself to think. For me, marriage would be about something that made sense because love made no sense. My head told me that you made no sense. You were just so damned young, you wore your heart on your sleeve, you were looking for the same happy-ever-after ending my mother believed in—the same happy ever ending I had no time for. I had built my box and I had no intention of stepping out of it, even though I knew you wanted me to. Am I losing you?'

He shot her the ghost of a fleeting smile that made her world tilt on its axis.

'I'm following you and you're right—I didn't understand, not really. Plus I was, well, I've never been that secure about my looks and I was...'

'Jealous?'

'No. Yes. Maybe.'

'Just maybe? Because I've been eaten up with jealousy thinking about all those men you might have been seeing behind my back in the last week or two.'

Milly's heart soared. She wondered whether she was hearing correctly. She half-leaned forward just in case she missed something and that devastating smile broadened as he read her mind.

'You can't let go, and I'm sorry about that, but...but you don't have to explain.'

'I do, my Milly, because I find that I let go a long time ago. I never realised it because I was just waiting in a holding bay for the right woman to come along and mess with my heart.'

The silence stretched between them. When she finally extended her hand along the table and he linked his fingers through hers, she experienced a rush of so many emotions, all vying for prominence, that she felt faint.

'I ran scared when you told me how you felt. I didn't know how to deal with it, Milly. And yet, I couldn't bring myself to tell my mother that it was over between us. I had the strangest feeling that if I said it out loud, if I vocalised it, then I would find myself in a place of no return. I couldn't face the thought of losing you but I didn't know how to make it right between us. My head was still waging war with my heart. The fact is, I love you. I was falling in love and I didn't even recognise the symptoms because I was so stubbornly and arrogantly convinced that I was immune.'

He absently played with her fingers in a way that was thrillingly intimate. 'You came into my life and you woke me up, Milly of the not-red hair, and my life is nothing without you in it.'

'And I love you,' Milly said with wrenching earnestness. 'I never loved Robbie, but you knew that, didn't you? When I think of what my life could have been if I hadn't found out the truth…' She shivered. 'I didn't want to fall in love with you either,' she admitted. 'I know you think I'm a hopeless romantic…'

'You are and I thank God for that.'

'But I still knew that you weren't a good bet and I was still fighting my own silly demons; still thought that you were just, well, that you'd never look at someone like me. Even though…' she dimpled at him '…you cured me of that.'

'Would you have felt that if I had continued being a harmless ski instructor?'

'You're never harmless and why, out of interest, didn't you tell me your true identity from the start?'

'It was liberating. You had landed there, like someone from a different planet, no airs, no graces and no knowledge of just how wealthy I was. You fascinated me from the very first moment I met you. And now, here we are. You are the love of my life, Milly, and I can't imagine life without you in it.'

'Okay.'

Lucas laughed. 'Is that all you have to say? When you're usually a woman of so many words?'

Milly grinned. 'I'm full of surprises.'

'And I want to be the one to find them all out, every day, for the rest of my life. Will you marry me? I'm asking that on behalf of both me and my mother…'

Milly laughed and rose, moving to sit on his lap so that she could feel his arms around her, holding her close, never letting her go.

'In that case, since you've brought your mother into the equation, what can a girl do but accept?'

* * * * *

MILLS & BOON®

Seven Sexy Sins!

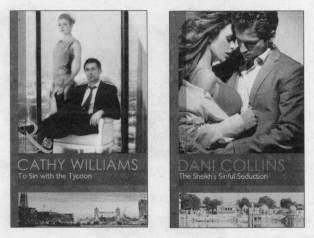

The true taste of temptation!

From greed to gluttony, lust to envy, these fabulous stories explore what seven sexy sins mean in the twenty-first century!

Whether pride goes before a fall, or wrath leads to a passion that consumes entirely, one thing is certain: the road to true love has never been more enticing.

Collect all seven at
www.millsandboon.co.uk/SexySins

MILLS & BOON®

MODERN™

POWER, PASSION AND IRRESISTIBLE TEMPTATION